Vault

David Rose was born in 1949, living outside West London, between Windsor and Richmond. He spent his working life in the Post Office. His debut story was published in *The Literary Review*, and since then he has been widely published by small presses in the UK and Canada. He was joint owner and Fiction Editor of *Main Street Journal*.

Also by David Rose

Vault

DAVID ROSE

SALT

CROMER

PUBLISHED BY SALT

12 Norwich Road, Cromer, Norfolk NR27 0AX United Kingdom

© David Rose, 2011, 2013

Printed and bound in the United Kingdom by Lightning Source UK Ltd

Typeset in Paperback 9.5./13.5

ISBN 978 1 907773 11 2 paperback

1 3 5 7 9 8 6 4 2

Vault is dedicated to the staff of Pizza Express, Staines,
where it was written, in my lunch hours.

Vault

1a

Across a lunar plain a dot is moving, weaving and skidding around the crumbling track, skirting rain-filled potholes flaring in the lurid light. Its speed from this height is difficult to estimate. From a lower perspective it would seem to average twenty mph, allowing for the detours.

From a yet lower point of view, ground level from the rear, it is silhouetted against the flat horizon. Despite the swerves the legs maintain a piston rhythm below the hump.

As the road twists we see it side on, just make out in the slanted sun the spokes, their sparkle dulled by dust carefully smoothed onto axle grease. The hump doubles, separates, as we distinguish haversack from spine. Drop handlebars like downturned horns.

The road turns back and it is headed into the quenching sun. The streaming clouds lidding down the last rays are smoke-smudged in places, until they merge completely with the dust haze in the south.

Occasionally, with retarded noise, the haze is added to

by discrete plumes, bursts of dust in the middle distance.
They do not impede the pace of the cyclist . . .

1b

CHIRON, FOR CHRIST's sake. Look, alright, yes, the bike becomes a part of you, if you're a natural, even if you're not, providing you're professional. But Chiron? For God's sake.

For me it wasn't so much a case of being a natural as of simply having been born on a bike. Almost literally.

My parents met on bikes — a collision, in fact, on a Sunday club run — courted on bikes, went down the aisle to a saluted arch of wheels, and honeymooned on a CTA youth hostel tour, on which I was presumably conceived.

My mother, having spent the last months of pregnancy grounded, insisted on some form of accommodation for me immediately after birth. Fortunately I *piston* was a summer baby. My father bought a second-hand pushchair, cut off the handle and bolted the handle-stays to his seat post. He would ride in front, my mother behind, riding shotgun.

As I grew older I was given a flag to wave, although at that time there were very few cars even on the arterial roads of the Southeast. If I did see a car, I would wave the flag more in excitement than warning.

As I grew too big for the trolley, my father was offered a sidecar by a grateful patient, and adapted it, but it was too heavy for a bike so he bought a tandem. Cornering with the sidecar I gather was difficult, because he rigged up a brake on the side-car itself, with a lever of its own, which I was trained to yank hard whenever he yelled.

But on a straight run they built up speed and I could watch the hedgerows whizzing past as I rang my bell.

Then my own first bike. Second-hand and anonymous — the frame transfers had been painted over several times. Even with the saddle at its lowest I couldn't reach the pedals; my father put wooden blocks on them to raise them two inches. But it was mine.

They sold the tandem so we could go back to formation — my father, me, mother in the rear, protective. In allowance for my short legs, they held back, much to my annoyance. I wanted to stretch out, see the hedgerows retreat at the same dizzying pace as before.

That didn't happen until my first new bike — a Sprite Junior — and I was allowed to head the formation. Briefly, for by then my mother was showing signs of the illness that would invalid her and rather than slow us up, she sold her bike and allowed her club membership to lapse.

My father and I then rode together side by side, or leapfrogged each other to stretch our lungs.

Then, with a growing practice and my mother to look after, he too dropped out. I was on my own, setting my own pace.

I liked that at first. But I began to feel lonely. So I joined a club.

Look, all of this matters. I can't explain why, but it does. I mentioned it in the radio interview. He could have checked. Novelists are supposed to research the background, aren't they?

An ordinary pre-war childhood, like thousands of others. I didn't come from nowhere. I'm certainly not a bloody centaur.

So, as I said, I joined Surrey Olympians. I suppose I found in them a substitute family on club runs, but more than that—a camaraderie I hadn't known I was looking for, combining both support and competitiveness, ésprit de corps and scope for glory.

No, *glory* is not right. It's a more private achievement, a measuring of oneself, but not against others. I can't explain, but it's significant that I performed better in time trials than on the track. Yourself against the clock. No distractions. Comparison with others' times comes later, after the event, when it no longer matters.

One course I remember in particular, a ten-mile course we used in the evenings. It involved a sharp bend followed immediately by a steep climb. The first time I rode it I was unprepared for the climb, stuck in too high a gear, with the incline too steep to change down. I struggled to reach the top, out of the saddle, treading the pedals, almost immobile at one point, ready to dismount. I made it, though. My worst time ever for a ten.

That course became my personal testing ground. I finally did some of my best times on it. And it helped uncover my talent for climbing.

Concentrate on your strengths — always been my motto. I began to train on Box Hill in the evenings and on Saturdays. I'd reckon to climb it twice a session, three times on a Saturday. My legs would be jelly on the way home, ribs aching, lungs seared. But I'd learnt technique, pacing, posture, and bloody-mindedness.

It paid off. I sought out courses with climbs in them, the steeper the better. There weren't many of them in the Southeast, and I couldn't travel far, but on courses like the Hog's Back I was unbeatable. On flat courses, out-standingly mediocre.

In 1942, I think, Percy Stallard initiated the return of massed-start road races. Most of our depleted club decided to try it. I wasn't keen. It meant learning new skills, new thinking: riding in a bunch, holding a wheel, taking turns at the head of a break. Simply being among others instead of out on my own against the watch.

Only on a race with a series of hills did I come into my own, breaking away on the first climb, keeping the lead on the descent, holding it on the flat to the next climb. I was sure to be caught over several miles of flat. But on one occasion, I wasn't. I think I had demoralised them. I finished nearly two minutes ahead of the bunch.

But it was only the once.

When my call-up came, I almost welcomed it.

2a

HE VEERS OFF the road, swings off the bike, pulls out a blotched tarpaulin from his haversack and flaps it over the lain-down bike. He crawls under the tarpaulin himself.

His fingers slide along the crossbar, locate the buckles and undo the straps. The rifle drops free. He checks and double-checks it. He crabs across to the edge of the tarpaulin, rolls twice and stretches behind the snaggled course of a drystone wall. Slowly he scrabbles away the stone-dust, removes a stone to open a gap, rechecks the angle of shadow, and eases the barrel through the gap. He squints through the telescopic sight, finds his range, rechecks the bolt.

And waits.

Dry rustle of wind in grass. The spool of a woodlark high in the cloud. A distant scream. Curlicues of sound against the ground-bass of far-off artillery.

Faint crack and sigh as the warm stone contracts.

Call of an early owl.

Now: rasp of a shot bolt, long-drawn wheeze of hinges. Two figures emerge from the lower half of a barn door, stooping, blundering forward, a pantomime horse costumeless. They straighten cautiously beside a tree. Officer and aide. Which is which? Field glasses raised. But by which one? Fifty-fifty chance if he guesses. Not good enough odds.

He looks through his spotting scope. The field glasses are Zeiss, non-standard issue. The soldier's own? That's the officer, then.

He waits. His breathing's down to hibernation level.

The glasses emerge further from behind the tree, begin to pan. He waits until they catch the low-angled light, aims six inches below the flash, fires.

The glasses jerk up, fall back, momentarily catching the light again. An arm embraces the trunk, slips slowly down.

Already he's rolled back under the tarpaulin, clinching the straps round the rifle, collapsing the telescope into its case. He listens for the bang of the barn door, scrape of the bolt.

He snatches and bunches the tarpaulin, stuffs the rucksack, lifts and runs the bike to the road, scoots and mounts.

He freewheels into camp, swings off and brakes in one easy movement. Others stand aside as he pushes his bike, one hand on the saddle, leans it into a hedge.

They greet him, but with reserve, grudged respect, downplaying his difference but acknowledging it in doing so.

He *feels* different; knows he stands out. He tells himself it's in *looking* different: the hand-tailored suit of sack hessian, grass-dyed; consciously suppresses a swagger that still shames him. He's handed a mug of tea, accepts with a nod, attempted smile, but the private has withdrawn, back to the group.

He takes his tea over to the hedge, sits by his bike, filing a nick into his rifle stock.

Taking a spanner from his saddlebag, he takes off one pedal, strips and de-grits the bearings, screws back the pedal.

He lies back on one arm, spinning the pedal, pleased by its run, its freeness, until he's called to report.

2b

IT WASN'T RESPECT, grudging or otherwise, they felt. It was uneasiness. The feeling was that there was something sneaky about shooting a man you could see, that it wasn't quite cricket.

We were pariahs, reminders of the job we all had to do, in its barest terms.

I at least had the consolation of logic. The revulsion of killing a single man, having had him in your sights for several minutes, the idea that it was better to kill men you couldn't see, *en masse* preferably, was to me irrational. I at least killed them cleanly, outright. Professional pride, of course, but humane too, objectively.

But none of that really eased the loneliness.

Look, no one becomes a loner by choice. You react in certain ways to the circumstances you're in. And those reactions shape the rest of your life.

Shall I tell you why I volunteered for sniper duties? Trench funk. Pure and simple.

In training, on Salisbury Plain, we had to dig in, and were then subjected to a constant barrage for three hours.

They made it as realistic as possible. But we knew the real thing would be different, and much worse. But even without the bombing I was getting claustrophobic.

I knew then I wouldn't be able to face it. You're not in control, the adrenalin *dry rustle* pumps, but you can't channel it. I decided then that I wanted to be more in control of my own destiny, my own death if necessary. Rather take my chances by myself, be responsible to and for myself.

So I put in for the training course at Bisley. Three weeks with the Lovats. Most were Scots, gamekeepers, gillies, a few of them poachers. All born with hunting rifles in their hands.

There were certain myths surrounding us because of that. That you had to have the hunting instinct, had to be a natural shot, have superhuman eyesight.

I had none of that, had only ever used a rifle at a funfair, and once on a clay pigeon shoot on a patient's estate. I wasn't a good shot, in their terms. I certainly had no hunting craft in my blood.

But in fact the most successful snipers weren't the most accurate shots at a thousand yards — they were the average shots who got closest to their targets. They weren't the *hunters*, merely the determined, the bloody-minded.

I was certainly bloody-minded. And I had to succeed, had to prove myself. I had a professional pride in my efficiency — as great as my father's in his diagnosis or surgery.

And I took risks.

But really, we weren't so much hunters as hunter-gatherers. Most of our time was spent, in fact, gathering — intelligence-collecting: forward gun emplacements, troop movements, ammunition dumps.

Hence the bike.

I came across it in the outhouse of the farm we had settled into. The farmer, or his son, had evidently been a keen cyclist before the invasion. It was expensive, well-oiled, well-maintained, or had been. It had dérailleur gears, which had never really caught on with clubmen in England before the war. They take a little practice in finding the gear, but I liked them, even on the flat terrain we were in.

The Germans at that time were some miles distant. We were spread fairly thin, transport was tied up. It was either several hours' slog, or use the bike. I opted for the bike. Certain to have been against regulations, but it made sense. I could get nearer to their lines than in a jeep. And if I did take a couple of potshots, I could be out of the way pretty quick. Barring punctures.

And the occasion when the gears were buggered. I had dropped the bike a bit abruptly to take cover, must have bent the dérailleur mech out of true. I potted two sentries and was planning to get the hell out. Couldn't find the gear. It was just like that first time trial, stuck in a big gear against the wind, having to get out of the saddle and tread the pedals, chain grating, feeling I was getting nowhere and waiting for the flak. Fortunately, they were too surprised to work out what had happened.

In a week we had moved on and I had had to leave the bike behind.

So it was hardly a consistent feature of my war.

Anyhow, I made it back to my pair, Swain, who had been covering me further back, with the scope, and we got back to position with the intelligence — we had been under some inaccurate shelling from a battery our artillery couldn't pin down.

As soon as we got back to position, it started — the snide remarks, the cold shoulders. Then the usual chap started up, started his needling.

Swain rose to it, started waving his rifle. It all got a bit ugly. I pushed between them, grabbed the barrel. The rifle went off, grazed my knee. It didn't seem much at the time, but it turned septic from the soil on my skin.

I was out of action for a few days, but it cleared up enough, although the chipped knee left me with a permanent limp.

Look, I know novelists like to deal in allusions, parallels, but that's all it was — an incident, and compared to Swain's death, shot out of a tree by a bazooka shell a few days later, a trivial one. It did, however, have repercussions I never expected at the time.

It also got me excused mortem duty. It was others, including some of the needlers, who had to search the undergrowth for Swain's body parts, assemble them for burial. I purposely avoided looking at the collected corpse, stood to attention at the grave, weight on one leg, remembering him alive. Then did my best to forget him. Friendships were expected to be short. Though, like a twin lost in childhood, he's been with me ever since.

3a

THEY EASED DOWN into the ditch, the ochreous water seeping osmotically up into the hessian, adding its stain to the camouflage. They each scooped mud by the handful from the bottom, smeared it over their faces, the water tickling down their necks, adding to the shiver. But the fragrance of the saturated sedge calmed him with a wave of warm nostalgia.

They didn't, after all, have long to wait. McKuen heard, or felt, the vibration of the troop carrier. He pressed himself closer against the clay.

It was almost past them now, but still too soon. He motioned Tusa to wait, wait. He counted, exhaling on each count, then nodded.

McKuen fired, hit the rear tyre as agreed. With the direction of the wind, the Germans may not have heard the shot, assumed it was a burst, were jumping down, looking at the wheel. They had a luxury of time to choose, aim.

He felt—for the first time, that he was aware of—the full extent of his power, of his decision of life or death over these distant strangers. He felt Godlike. Perhaps because of the choice, because he could select only a number from a grouped target, was not forced to shoot whatever presented itself to his sight.

He hoped Tusa and he hadn't selected the same target as he decided for the older, bearded soldier scratching his neck.

He watched the man slap his neck in surprise as the bullet pierced it, then crumple. Another, kneeling at the wheel, toppled synchronously. Obviously they hadn't duplicated targets.

They had time to down four more, then he gave the order to run, still doubled, along the ditch, boots cloying in the mud, back to the dog-leg bend, along to the bushes then out, hauling themselves up, sprinting across the open to the welcoming copse.

With yards to go, an opportunist shot rang across clearing, hitting Tusa in the shoulder, spinning and pitching him as he ran.

McKuen whisper-shouted: Stay down, lie still. He ran back to him, grabbed his other arm, dragged him sledge-like over the wet grass into the bracken of the wood. Three Germans, having recovered from the surprise, had leapt the ditch, were cutting diagonally across the open.

He dropped beside Tusa, pulled a branch round to steady his rifle, aimed across the trajectory of their chase, allowing the first to run into his sights, and fired. The second swerved but too late. The last, puffing behind, crouched and aimed. His shot went wild as he recoiled from the bullet smashing his ribcage.

It was quiet now. The birds were resettling in the trees.

He motioned Tusa up, held him, weakening, under his good arm, moved deeper into the wood, found a hollow.

He ripped the hessian, unbuttoned Tusa's jacket, felt the wound. The bullet had exited but not cleanly. He plastered his handkerchief over the shoulder, told Tusa to hold it on tight. Then he moved off, searching, through the undergrowth, on his knees.

He found a plant, stripped off the leaves, leaving the stem a whip quivering, searched on, like Linnaeus on a field trip.

He spotted the other plant he needed in a stand of nettles, plunged his hand in and pulled the plant out by the root.

He crawled back to Tusa.

He layered the leaves of each plant into a herbal sandwich, rubbed them between the heels of his hands to bruise them, carefully eased the poultice over the entry wound, made another for the exit wound, bound them with the ripped handkerchief and told Tusa to hold his hand over them for as long as possible.

He rolled the remainder of the leaves into a wad and put it into his ration tin.

It was still quiet, but McKuen knew another troop

carrier would be along shortly. Their own platoon would have moved position by now, would still be digging in. They would need more time.

He ran across the clearing to the dead Germans, pat-searched their greatcoats, found what he was looking for, and ran back to Tusa.

He said: Are you fit enough to climb trees? Tusa nodded. They moved back out to the copse. He found a beech with a low fork, hunched over for Tusa to mount his shoulders, pushed up. Tusa gripped the branch one-handed, heaved himself up into the fork, inched higher, straddling the branch, until he was in the thick of the foliage.

McKuen ran back across to the ditch, crept along it to within yards of the deserted carrier.

The rumble started within minutes. He waited for it to slow as they saw the first carrier, pulled the pin of the grenade, counted, and with his arm up through a tussock of grass, rolled it, marble-like, under where he reckoned the lorry to be, pulled the pin of the second, rolled it a little harder, pressed himself into the mud of the ditch.

He felt the first explosion lift the lorry then mushroom as it exploded the fuel tank. Then the third, from the far side of the road — the second grenade.

He could hear from the commotion that several, at least, of the troops aboard had survived, probably thrown clear.

He stayed exactly where he was.

He heard the thuds as they jumped the ditch. They had evidently seen the corpses, assumed that was the direction they were being shelled from. He wasn't sure how many there were.

Then a shot rang out from the copse, followed by three more at comfortable intervals.

Then silence.

3b

So now i'm Machaon. Can't he make up his bloody mind?

Look, they were just dock leaves, to soothe the wound. I wasn't ever a herbalist. And although, yes, I had been destined for medical school until the war started, I hadn't learnt anything from my father, had only occasionally seen him at work.

You do the best you can in the circumstances you're in. And as to Fateful intervention, you pick whichever targets you're most likely to hit.

I did what had to be done, the only thing I could do. The latitude in any situation, any aim, is limited. And my aim at the time was to delay the Germans long *quivering* enough for the men to dig in. Then, to get Rance — his name was Rance — and myself back to the battalion as soon as possible, get his wound cleaned properly.

Which took us a while. We had to make a wide detour, across open ground, partly crawling, with a bush apiece netted to our backs. When dark came, Rance could *only* crawl, he was so weak. I helped him up, and we staggered the last few miles like a pair of drunks in a three-legged race.

Battalion had found themselves a nice farmstead, were well ensconced. The medics patched up Rance's shoulder, but his sniping duties were over. After a couple of weeks they transferred him to an artillery division.

I was told I'd been cited for the Military Medal. I insisted either we both got it or neither.

Alright, it sounded heroic in retrospect. At the time, it's more complicated. Yes, part of you is playing the hero, acting the part. Part of you just gets on with the job, looking forward to a hot mug of tea, the chance to relax your nerves. You have to remember how young we were, remember . . . But either way, we didn't think in terms of medals. Their award was too arbitrary, capricious, even.

In the event, I didn't get mine. The report came to light of the incident, the accident, when I intervened in the fight with Swain. It hinted at the possibility of deliberate self-infliction. A subtle variant of shooting yourself in the foot. They took the hint.

Rance, I'm pleased to say, got his.

I was back out alone again, which suited me fine. Sometimes on a bright night I'd go out, settle myself in a hollow or behind a hedge, see what appeared — a lone Jerry heading for the latrines, an early sniper setting out.

Mostly there was nothing. I'd look up at the moon, drink the frost-weighted air, smell the mud.

I'd make a wide detour back, to tire myself. I relied on fatigue to dull my nerves, the sharpness of being alive.

During the day it wasn't so bad. There was the possibility of being spotted, even a stray shell. The odds were fluid, but the possibility was there, of an end to all the absurdity, the uncertainty. The raggedness.

No Man's Land. That, I think, was the point of being a sniper. You *lived* in No Man's Land.

Maybe news of the citation had leaked out, but anyway after our delaying operation, there was a warmth, a cordiality toward us for a while. But it no longer mattered to me.

As the advance on Germany pushed through, we were moved north, into Holland. Often our movement paralleled the Germans', with only a canal between us.

Both sides now deployed snipers in large numbers. We were suddenly in favour.

For some of us it became like a Wild West duel: we got to know our opposite numbers, recognised their methods, favourite hides, even their personal habits, routines, latrine breaks. We earmarked them for ourselves, our personal quarry, as a point of honour.

Mine — one of them — I stalked for days. We were either side of a canal, a distance of around five hundred yards, both keeping to the rubble and beams of the flattened warehouses. We returned shots several times.

I learnt to recognise him from his smell. It was distinctive. They, like us, probably hadn't washed in weeks, but this was different. I never found out what it was — his diet, some medical problem, or maybe simply that he used horse dung as camouflage. I don't know. Whatever it was, I could tell, if the wind was right, that he was staked out there somewhere. It was just a matter of waiting, to see whose nerve failed first, who shot first.

I embedded the neck of a broken bottle in a pile of rubble, so when it caught the light it could be mistaken for a rifle sight. He fell for it eventually, couldn't resist. As much curiosity as anything, perhaps.

I had been watching his most likely position from fifty yards down the canal. I waited as he eased round a coil of rusted chain, worked his rifle barrel through the links. Then he turned his head, to check the wind, maybe. I could see the back of his head, his neck. His hair was short, shaved. He had jug ears, at least the one I could see, and behind it his head was white, where he had camouflaged only the front of his ear.

I aimed at that spot behind the jug ear, waited for him to fire. He was taking his time. He looked younger then than he must actually have been — looked, in fact, no

24

older than ten, I suppose due to the haircut and jug ear. Anyway, as he tightened on the trigger, I brought the bead down, hit him through the arm, the bicep.

It would have been like shooting a baby. I put it down to recoil—his shot went off as mine hit him—notched it up as usual.

I found myself thinking of home just after that—my father, friends, club mates. I hadn't thought of them in months. It's a different world, and the two don't mesh. You have to live in one or the other. Abandon hope when you cross the Channel, enter the tunnel. Of course, I hadn't read Dante then.

I began to think for the first time of why we were there, what we were doing, relating it to home and future, and all the things we were meant to be fighting for, and against. Then I forgot it, got on with the job. Limited objective, limited horizon. It was the only way to function.

I seemed then to have been always in the war, and always in No Man's Land.

4a

MCKUEN CRAWLING THROUGH the rubble, carefully shifting broken beams, twisted girders, serpentining then coiling, senses alert to every noise, every scent carried across the oil-skimmed water, rifle gripped in his crooked arm, binoculars swung onto his horizontal back, the strap cutting into his throat at every move.

He reaches the stub of wall fifty yards from the canal's edge, crouches in, settles himself. Checks his rifle, snaps in the clip, uncaps his binoculars, shakes out his camouflage cloth. An hour to sun-up. He breaks his last squares of chocolate, puts one into his mouth, resisting the impulse to chew, letting it melt behind his teeth.

He switches his consciousness to automatic pilot, prepares to wait, oscillating between the purely mental, purely animal. His instinct now filters the sensory information borne on the wind.

As the sun warms the ground the odours richen: rusted metal, dank water metallic and sour, crushed weed. Something drops into the water—he tenses. Maybe a water rat; not a fish—they are floating on the surface, concussed from the shelling. A crow hops across the earth, prospecting the shaled floor, gives up, flaps, clacking, into the air, leaving the silence eddying.

McKuen stiffens, returns to tingling consciousness. He lifts the edge of the camouflage cloth higher above his nostrils, tests the air. He scents him, as the breeze quickens, scents the adversary, his odour fading up from the olfactory background, tuning in from the white noise. There's no mistaking the fingerprint odour. He has scented him down, scented him in his lair.

McKuen is barely breathing now, watching, the blood-scent stronger by the minute. The German is slowly panning his binoculars, stops, backtracks, is pre-occupied now with the rubble heap, the glinting glass, undecided. He lowers the binoculars, waits, takes them up again. His skin is crawling though he is bodily motionless. The light's in his favour, but has he been seen?

Finally his nerve gives, he decides on an exploratory shot. He works his rifle through the rusted links, manoeuvring so the sight lines up through the next coil's chink. Targets in on the glint of glass, holds back to synchronise the movement of lungs and shoulder. Tightens on the trigger.

McKuen has him locked on now, has taken all the time he has needed. He's there in his cross hairs, the patch of white, bare nape, vulnerable as a shelled snail. McKuen feels the surge of omnipotence. He holds the knife to the life-thread. He starts to sport, mentally tossing a coin.

Fractionally adjusts his aim.

Rips off the arm, like a spider's leg, setting off the secondary shock of the German's gun as the arm jerks and tears.

McKuen watches him roll and huddle behind the chains, watches his other arm slither across to finger the rifle butt, dragging it back, can hear his excruciation.

He starts to pack his things and withdraw.

5a

We'll hang out the washing on the Siegfried line.
Have you any dirty washing, mother dear?

THE BUILD-UP HAS started, the armies are massing at
the ramparts, balked by the fortifications — each fort, of
six feet of concrete, surrounded by a moat, approached
by a causeway criss-crossed by the sightlines of pillbox
emplacements, equally impervious to cannon, artillery,
aerial bombardment. The only way is to breach from the
rear by an infantry attack.

For the time being, the armies are keeping their distance, adapting their tactics.

The first consideration is the pillboxes.

McKuen, with a dozen other snipers on secondment
from wherever they can be found, are gauging the angles,
settling themselves in under the protection of air fire.
Meanwhile the artillery are likewise calculating range and
trajectory, to cover the rear entry routes to the pillboxes.
Tanks and infantry are tensed for attack.

On the radioed signal the snipers start, taking their

time, picking off the machine-gunners in the concrete tombs, as the artillery and aircraft keep back their replacements.

After forty minutes a tank moves forward to test the response. Sporadic, lop-sided machine gun fire, but the criss-cross pattern is ragged, abbreviate.

The order is given, and the tanks race in single file across the causeway, followed by the first wave of infantry with wire-cutters to strip back the barbed wire frills round the dragon's teeth for the full surge of soldiers, bayonets fixed.

Under a protective hail from the tanks, they drop incendiary down the ventilation shafts while sappers charge and blow the casements of the rolled steel doors.

Internal resistance is minimal — the defenders, those unburnt, surrender, come up from the depths with hands on heads.

By mid-afternoon the fort is taken, the first breach of the impregnable walls.

Now the milling convoys, unstrained, rush through, beginning their sweep across the windy plains.

5b

Hasn't he checked *any* of the history?

It was the Americans, under Patton, who pierced the Siegfried Line, in the west. We were to outflank the Line in the north, over the Dutch border, mop up the pillboxes from the rear. It wasn't quite that simple.

They had extended the Siegfried defences along the Dutch border to the North Sea, though not as securely as the original Line. We had to use the gaps. But the gaps included marshes, and the heavily wooded Reichswald.

We snipers came into our own on the marshes. Trenches were out of the question, but cover for us was adequate, lying on a tarpaulin over a few planks, with the grass and reeds covering us entirely. Working in teams we could pick off a battery before they could even find our range, then move *teeth* on, dragging the boards like a sleigh.

We gave up counting our bag.

In the Reichswald it was different. We were redundant.

Mile after mile of uniformly spaced trees, continuously shelled from beyond the wood with shells designed to explode in the branches. Nothing we could fire at, no clearing to give us a range.

We lumped in with the rest of the infantry, slogged our way through with no tank cover, just rifles and grenades.

Dante's wood had nothing on this — this was the depths of the inferno. A solid ceiling of overhead branches keeping out the light, and which any time could rain down hot metal and broken branches. Constant fear of ambushes.

Nights were even worse. We couldn't bed down, or keep dry in the rain. And when it didn't rain, the frost in the split branches would set up a crackling at every breeze that spooked the most phlegmatic of us.

We got through. Most of us. Turned south and worked our way between the Siegfried Line and the Rhine, taking out the pillboxes as we went, which were mostly now unmanned anyway, being defenceless from the rear. They had dug themselves trenches by the side instead, so there was work for us, softening them up with sniper fire before the rest went in with grenades and machine guns.

After that, our role, the sniper's, was mostly rear-guard, defensive, spotting and radioing any counter-movements from behind, flushing out German snipers left on the out-skirts, preventing, in theory, any looting by either side of provisions earmarked for later collection. Then the dash to catch up.

It was in some ways the most disheartening time of all. The devastation was more thorough, more systematic, and I was part of it, although I could in my heart distance myself—my war was still one to one, I still had control over whom I shot, could ignore civilians, even looters, justify my conscience, such as it was.

But the thoroughness of the destruction couldn't be avoided. Towns flattened for miles, those civilians unable to flee living as troglodytes in cellars half-flooded with rain and sewage, making hopscotch forays to find crusts or cabbage leaves in the rubbled gutters. Surrender did them little good, as we were advancing too fast to stop and help beyond throwing rations from the convoys.

In many cases surrender cost them their lives. I remember coming more than once on town squares decorated with hanged civilians draped in white—sheets, bedspreads, whatever they'd used to signal with—victims of SS troops stationed or passing through.

In one instance the corpses were dangling barefooted, their shoes looted by their neighbours. I stared at the feet of one—man or woman, it was difficult to tell, especially farm workers—but old, anyway; stared at the hammer toe, yellowed corns, uncut nails brittlely chipped. I determined then to return, whenever the war was over.

Meanwhile we pushed on, finding the resistance was coming from younger and younger soldiers, schoolboys with a kamikaze desire to prove their patriotism while they still had the chance.

No food, but as much ammunition, as many *panzerfausts*, grenades, bullets as they could drag or carry.

Up to, even after the formal surrender, there were enclaves of boys and raggedly-determined survivors mounting ambushes in woods and once-tilled fields, or networks of sewers in the towns.

We tried, as far as our lives were in no danger, to ignore them or disarm them. To extend the killing seemed pointless. We just hadn't the stomach for it now. The full surrender produced a feeling of profound anticlimax. And the exhaustion, overnight, had caught up with us.

6a

HE HAS COME through, when so many have not. He wears lightly his bright invincibility.

There have been spontaneous celebrations, improvised with whatever drink was to be had, in whatever places they found themselves in, speeches of thanks by commanding officers, prayers and joshing.

His platoon has come across a village almost unharmed, still intact, have commandeered houses, their inhabitants confined to outhouses and cellars. Now they can celebrate more leisurely, allow the slow return of mortal emotions.

The first miracle is a shower with hot running water, and all in turn stand and douse in the exquisite jets, step out into towels offered by the daughters of the house, willing slaves out of relief at the soldiers' not being Russians, who are still to the east.

They offer clean linen, hot coffee, stoke the stove.

McKuen relaxes into himself.

Then come the libations—spiced wine, beer, roasted pig, freshly slaughtered, anointed with honey so the crackling is sweet. The daughters, hovering behind the couches as beneficent skivvies, quick to replenish and withdraw.

Having satisfied themselves with food and drink, they bed down, under duckdown quilts, and sleep, fitfully at first out of years' long habit, but drifting deeper and deeper until fully submerged.

A morning patrol in light drizzle takes them out of the village into man-plowed fields and scattered copses. Now, like town dwellers in the country for the first time, they are disturbed by the noise, the negative noise, the hum of silence with no groundbass, no backlight of artillery, only the creak of the earth, whisper of leaves, whenever they stop.

So the whistle reaches them ahead of the shell and they cram to the floor as the *panzerfaust* passes and detonates in the field behind. They swing out of the jeep and belly-flop onto the grass.

Only McKuen can see the werewolf in the trees. He points out the copse, asks for a burst of machine gun fire into the treetops while he finds a support, fixes the range. He gambles on there being only the one, a lone act of frenzy or hate, the one in his sights, an ex-Para-boy of maybe sixteen. Not even a helmet, only fur-eared cap, such is his contempt or trust.

McKuen takes his time as the boy peers through the undergrowth, wanting this to be the most accurate shot of his war, sends the bullet through the top of the cap to lift it off the Para-boy's head, earflaps flapping, and as it flutters down, puts a second bullet through it, to complete the humiliation.

Another burst of machine gun fire and they get back into the jeep, complete the patrol.

6a(b)

'WELL, YOU CAME out of it alive then, I thank the Lord. No shell shock? How's the knee?'

'It's fine unless it stiffens. It's true what they say, you can feel the weather changing.'

'Shall I just take a look at it for you?'

'No, it's fine, really. The MO was good, thorough. You'd have got on.'

'You'd rather wear your wounds with pride, then? You have the right, I suppose. I suppose war must change people, it's to be expected. Look, it's a little early maybe to ask, but have you thought what you want to do now? Will it be medical school, after all? Have you thought?'

'No, I've no plans. Just reacclimatize to begin with.'

'Well, it's early days yet. Settle yourself down first.

By the way, I had a letter from a friend of yours, a Mr. Tusa. Addressed to the hospital, but they forwarded it. He was awarded the MM, I gather. He seemed apologetic. Seemed to think he'd got yours by mistake. Wanted me to know.'

'Did he mention his shoulder?'

'He didn't speak of it. I suppose that's the code again?

It won't help we doctors, though, when the latent problems appear. You really ought to have a good overhaul, you know. Wouldn't take me long.'

'I'm fine. Really.'

He's out walking the family dog, although not the one he remembers, which is dead. Every afternoon walking the common, noting the slow encroachment of the gravel pits, instinctively matching his eyesight with the springer's as he flings the quoit, gauging the wind from the scent, the height of the skylark from its song, moving still in the present, the concentrated *now*.

It's a hard habit to break, and he doesn't wish to.

Eventually, he knows, he must. Knows that past and future will hinge open in an instant into sweeping planes, tilting dizzyingly, horizons streaking away, leaving him exposed, naked, among the multiplying choices.

He needs to cast his shadow, see it striding before or behind, visible to him if no one else. But to cast a shadow he needs sun, and space, light and room to manoeuvre, to act. Here the sun drains through watery cloud, obstacles impede — family feeling, social obligations, friendships already withered from the years' neglect.

The choice he makes is the only one open to him, thus bestowing the fullest freedom.

'Dad, if you really want to help . . .'

7a

I FELT VERY LOST on my return home — empty, isolated. My father was sympathetic, but for all his medical experience and professional empathy, didn't really understand. And it didn't much matter that he didn't.

Yet I still felt some need to be among those who did, who shared the assumptions of suffering.

It was one of the reasons I returned to the Continent, in addition to my original idea of being of help. I'm not sure that atonement was a concept I would have understood at the time, but in retrospect, that too was an element.

I had heard of several charities — aid and relief organisations — operating *shadow* across Europe, but I felt I couldn't be involved with those, couldn't handle the red tape and discipline, having been to a large degree exempt as a sniper from communal action. I decided to go it alone, trust my judgment as to who were genuinely in need, who not.

My father was very helpful, once he'd got used to the idea of my leaving again. He was very tied up with my mother, who was by then in a life behind drawn curtains, emotionally clinging.

I avoided entering her room more often than duty dictated. There was an oppressive scent of gardenias, with, I now guess, a base note of carbolic. The gardenia must have been perfume; I never saw any flowers.

She was always pleased to see me, effusive at first, clutching my arm, staring into my face. Then gradually I'd fade from her attention, she'd start to look round for my father, and I'd feel free to leave.

I feel very sorry for my father now. I felt sorry for him then, but it was outweighed by discomfort.

I think more than anything it was his hands, his hands on my shoulders. He had a surgeon's fingers, a pianist's fingers, long, agile. But oddly fleshy palms, plump heels.

Those hands summed up for me the dual role he had taken on from the onset of my mother's illness — consciously acting as both father and mother to me. It wasn't what I wanted. I had a mother. And for a father I would have preferred a more Victorian model. You can never be friends, because you can never be equals.

The cycle trips together in my youth hadn't been so bad — there was a physical distance between us, a distance I could control. But at home I felt awkward, doubly so as I sensed he felt the same.

Looking back, I know he was doing his best. I realize too that he was probably in part relieved at my going away again, quite apart from the burden of my mother; that his offer of help was not entirely altruistic.

Food was rationed here — there was probably more food available over there, due to the aid agencies — but he secured for me a supply of medical stuff, basic medicines — vaccines, aspirin — bandages, splints, disinfectants.

I bought another bike, a heavy-duty tourer with sprung saddle, front and rear panniers, stuffed the tyres with newspaper against punctures, and packed up my parents' old CTC tent and stove and a minimum of food and comforts in my kit-bag and musette. Set off across the Channel again.

Once across, I usually managed to hitch lifts in aid convoys for most of the journey. I wore my Army jacket to travel in, which speeded up paperwork with the ICC officials, then took it off before any dealings with local civilians, the people I was there to help, especially Germans. I felt strongly at the time that they too, many of them, were as much victims as the others, the French, Dutch, Flemish still making their way back home from deportations east.

I cycled through the back roads and villages, which official aid was not yet reaching, searching ditches and hedgerows where many slept, offered what medical comfort was within my power, directing them to field stations in severe cases, encouraging Germans to overcome their reluctance, their fear of refusal.

I was just trying to help.

My supplies soon ran out, which meant going home to load up and return. For the next trip, I salvaged the old sidecar from the shed, clamped it to the tourer. It was unwieldy, especially loading it onto lorries in the event of a lift — it would take three of us to lift it — but I was able to more than double my capacity, double the length of my stay.

It was on my third tour that an incident occurred that changed my focus.

I assume, looking back, that this must have occurred before, often, but I had never seen it. Or maybe it was because they were now getting some nourishment, gathering energy, shaking off the apathy of exhaustion.

A group of refugees, ragged and still emaciated, were nonetheless attacking a couple of others, local Germans, middle-aged burger types, a little less emaciated but no match for the fury of the group, who were kicking them frenziedly as they huddled on the paving, clutching each other as if in the throes of copulation.

I pulled on my army jacket, thinking it might calm or frighten them, and ran over, but not until I forcibly dragged them off, one by one, did they let up the assault. Then they cowered back in some recognition of their dependency on Allied aid. I motioned for them to clear off. I think they expected me to arrest them, such was their conditioning to uniforms.

I prised apart the German couple, held out a pack of bandages to show I meant no harm, began to feel for broken limbs and signs of concussion. I found — I hoped — only bruising, and dabbed on witch hazel. But you could see bruising in their eyes, a shocked recognition of how the world now saw them.

They insisted I came back with them to their home — maybe to protect them, maybe in gratitude. They made me weak acorn coffee, and we sat in their kitchen round the (cold) tiled stove, in relatively companiable silence.

After another round of — I felt, rather grudging — thanks, I rode off.

I realised that incidents like that would now become more frequent, should have been expected earlier. And a few days later came another which mirrored the first.

An aid station had been set up in a village square, mostly doling out food and blankets, so far as I could see. Judging by their relative conditions, the assembled crowd comprised both local Germans and travelling refugees. They were all grouped in knots, families maybe, packing and dividing their allotments of food. The lorry was driving away as I reached the square.

As it disappeared, a murmur of resentment caught and spread through the crowd. Then, almost as one, the locals turned on the refugees, hitting, kicking, pulling from them whatever they had been given, swearing and shouting. I picked out one or two words I knew, enough to understand that the Germans were accusing the refugees of depriving them of aid meant for them.

I had seen people during the war fight to the death over a crust of bread. This I felt could be as serious. This time there was nothing I could do to intervene. I cycled off to find some official of the occupying police, but I knew the nearest ICC office was miles away; by the time I got there, got them to act, the incident would be over.

I had never felt so powerless.

Later, administering first aid to a straggle of limping Belgians, I felt almost resentful, betrayed. I began to rethink what I was doing over there.

When I got home, I asked my father for Rance's letter, wrote to him at the address he had given. Called in a favour.

7b

A CLUMP OF TREES, coppiced by mortar, is beginning
to grow back, putting out shoots low on the splintered
trunks. The sun is rising behind them. The leaves clutch
at the light.

Once there was a road, now a muddied track fringed
by bracken. A woman is approaching, pushing a handcart
piled with effects, utensils, clothes, a cuckoo clock. She is
weary, grimed but in good spirits, humming a folksong to
the child on her back.

From the bracken around the copse a figure emerges,
waits for her to pass, waits a little longer, then follows at
a distance. His serge greatcoat trails in the dust. He is
hooded, stooped and nimble, striding the shell holes at
the road's edge, stopping whenever the woman stops to
reshoulder the child or adjust the cart's strapping.

By the next crossroads is an empty cottage; roof beams
jagging, windows shattered, it is now a way-station for
any traveller who can bring his own comfort.

She is headed toward it, not planning to stop, wanting
to press on. She is aware, in some cerebral whorl, of

the hooded man, although she's not seen him, feels his animus, quickens her step, quickens the tune.

The sun's warmth bruises the bracken, releases its scent. She feels slightly nauseous, from its heaviness, her exhaustion.

She has passed the cottage, passed the crossroads. There's a shout behind her, running feet, then she's being jostled, then held, arms embracing the child and her body, then others, two, three, upending the cart, cutting the straps, hauling out the clock, which is placed on the grass, pulling out clothes, pans, a half loaf, a cabbage. She is telling herself not to struggle, not to crush the child, be calm, quiescent. But the animal smell from the arms around her stirs her nausea, she needs to vomit, leans and doubles to do so and the arms loosen and she feels the weight of the body pull then release. She unbalances and falls with the body slumping away to the side. She has hardly registered the distant crack, sees only the blood on the temple, the imploded bone.

She hears the second shot, a third, is aware of more falling bodies, of running legs through the bracken, of a bubbling groan, and now a frantic silence.

She waits, feeling the child safe on her back, whimpering, clutching her hair. She feels the sun's warmth as a safeness. Slowly she gets up.

She steps round the corpses, rights her cart, pushes it

free of the legs sprawled under it, wheels it a few yards, begins to slowly repack the contents, the mental inventory concentrating her mind. She winds the clock, three turns, listens. It's ticking comfortably. She loads it on top, swaddled in the clothes, criss-crosses the straps.

There is, as she suspects, no one about.

She begins to push, hum, restraining herself to a slow andante.

In her hometown, as in others, rumours will circulate of a hooded protector, an avenging angel in belted robes. Sightings are reported, many of them simultaneous and miles apart. Tussles over food or squatters' rights are broken off as protagonists and antagonists alike look round in fear. Reviving stragglers restrain their long-pent hatred, not knowing on whose side the angels are now.

But there come times when the angels are goaded. When the hatred is fanned by bravado, by a gambled challenge to the lightning bolt, an ethical testing of the gods' response. And each such incident ends in death — by beating, suffocation, stabbing, stoning . . .

For every intervention on the moral plane displaces its own weight, repercusses unforeseeably.

At each aid station he is on the alert.

A village crossroads. The Red Cross lorry driving away. He

melts out from the trees, in the shadow of the first cottages, takes his position with a clear view of the square.

A family running into the square, the children scampering to keep up, arriving too late, standing breathless, dazed with disappointment. A man, alone, instinctively tactful, hiding his milk, bread, carrots behind his back as he crosses the square.

He is challenged, accosted, by the father, pleaded with by the mother, to share his food, it is too much for one. But maybe he too has a family, aged parents. And they should have been earlier—he has waited for three hours in hot sunshine.

In their desperation they snatch at the food, lunge at him as he tries to back away, the father grabbing at his jacket, pulling it over his shoulders, punching his stomach. The man sinks to his knees, frees his arms from the sleeves, hugs his stomach.

Now he's reaching to his hip. Pulls a knife, rushes the man, who trips over one of the children, holds his leg above him to ward off the knife.

Now. The decision is to be made in the split-second infinity the gods are given. A choice that splinters, ramifies through time, spreads through decades.

A choice between an elderly couple starving in a barn, or two children fatherless? A belated accounting for a surviving aggressor, or ironic compounding of victimhood?

Now the knife spins in the stark light, a blinding point revolving through the years.

8a

I HAD HANDED IN my own rifle at the end of the war. Somehow, I felt Rance would have found a way of keeping his. I was right. It cost me, of course.

I was tempted to invite him to join me, reconstitute our old teamwork. But I couldn't be entirely sure of his motives or actions if he accepted, so I let it go, just said I needed it to protect myself from revenge attacks by embittered ex-soldiers. He had, besides, met a girl he was serious about (not an adjective I would have applied to him before). He told me I should do the same.

What I told him wasn't entirely untrue. Word had spread of an Englishman tending the sick from a bicycle (some versions had it a motorbike, because of the sidecar, I suppose — others said a horse). But that, as far as I was aware then, was the extent of my notoriety. All this legend nonsense is novelism. Likewise the incidents he describes — fiction. It wasn't like that, didn't feel like that.

But nobody likes to see bullying. They'd step in, put a stop to it if they could. It's the normal reaction. And we have, eventually, to accept the consequences *clock* of our actions precisely because they are not predictable. The alternative is to give up on life altogether.

Look, there were transit camps, further east mostly, that had to be guarded by British troops, guarded from the inmates. They were Poles and Russians. They hated each other's guts.

They were united only in their hatred of Germans. They'd been mounting reprisal attacks on the refugees from Dresden, Berlin, Cologne . . . Should they have been left to it? Dump the blankets and bread and leave them all to fight it out? You have to act, however naively.

The greatcoat I retrieved from a scarecrow. It wasn't so much a disguise, it just hid the rifle. I kept them both in the sidecar under the bandages.

It's true I learnt to anticipate likely flashpoints. In most cases a shout and wave of the gun was enough. Occasionally a warning shot. In a few instances I had to shoot to wound. I was still a marksman, after all. Although I wouldn't claim I was capable of shooting a knife out of man's hand at six hundred yards, if that's what he meant to imply. Or was the man killed? Novelists love obscurity.

I only killed once.

I tended a woman—hardly more than a girl, although she turned out to be older than she looked, an impression given by an absence in her eyes, a staring apathy that made her seem a child—who was half-marching, half-stumbling through the rubbled outskirts of a town.

She didn't respond to my call, hardly turned her head. I had to overtake and confront her, pointing to my medical bag, holding up a roll of bandage. She allowed herself to be led to my bike, where I spread a blanket on the roadside, started to examine her, bathe her feet. She had a duffel bag on her shoulder, which she swung round and cradled when she sat down. She volunteered nothing about herself, except to repeat softly *mütter, mütter.* I assumed she was travelling to find her mother, returning home, perhaps, on the loss of her home, husband.

She didn't appear to be hungry, even thirsty. I wondered if she was carrying sufficient food, and where she had obtained it. I gently took the duffel bag from her arms, disentangling the cord. She made no attempt to stop me, so I assumed there was nothing of personal value in it.

It contained a small bundle, a crumpled cardigan, I thought. I opened it up. It was a baby. It had been dead some days, by my guess.

I rewrapped it, put it back in the bag, gave it to her. She held it in her lap.

I allowed her to rest on the blanket while I took out the primus, brewed some tea.

She took the mug, sipped the tea like taking medicine, put the mug carefully down on a stone. Still without a word, she scrambled up, hoisted the duffel bag round on to her shoulder, marched away. I watched her as I folded the blanket, hung the primus on the pannier.

I gave her a good start then pedalled slowly behind her. We were heading away from the town into open farmland, now mostly weeded over.

Two figures emerged from a ditch, stood in the road awaiting her approach. She didn't take any notice, just kept marching. They fell in on either side of her, took her arms, slowed her down. She allowed herself to be led to the roadside, searched.

One of them took the bag, opened it, as I had done, with the same surprise. He too stuffed the corpse back into the bag, but then started to whirl it around by the cord, above his head.

By this time I had dismounted, taken out the rifle, had it aimed and cocked. I waited for him to let go of the cord, to see the bag arc and fall into the field. The woman was holding out her arms to snatch the bag. Instead of letting go, he caught the bag itself, threw it over her head to the other, who threw it back, playing piggy-in-the-middle.

That would have been enough for me. But they tired of this, held the bag out to her, then held her as she took it, pulled her down, began to rip at her clothes. She was not resisting, which to me made it worse.

I hit the first cleanly in the head. The other, when he realised, at first jumped up, then as quickly threw himself down. I hit him in the arm.

He stood up again, raised his other arm, looking round to find me. I called, so he could take my position, come to face me. He turned slowly, trying to pull up his injured arm.

I shot him through the chest.

The woman waited a moment, then picked up the bag and without a look back, carried on marching.

I was shaking as I put the rifle back in the sidecar, but, I realised, from anger, an anger I had never felt during the war itself.

I admit I felt too a sense of power, exercised in what I felt, knew, was a just cause, an almost vocational fulfillment. But a god? I never felt that.

Imagine yourself in that situation. Would you have felt any differently? Behaved differently?

Anyway, that was the incident that gave credence to the legend that was apparently already circulating. Actually it was two legends: that of the ministering angel on a bicycle, that of the hooded avenger (I never wore a hood). I found out about them later, in a book on the aftermath of the War in Europe. It made reference to the legends in its footnotes. Two separate footnotes. No one had connected them.

That, then, was the novel's legend—footnotes in an academic tome.

As it happened, someone *had* made the connection at the time. An official at some level of the ICC put two and two together.

I was picked up, escorted before a local board to explain my actions, mission, motives. They had no actual evidence, no eyewitness reports, only hearsay. Actually, I don't think they wanted to find evidence. Another decision to make, a case to open, loose ends . . . There were more pressing problems with millions, literally, on the move, repatriated, sometimes forcibly, embers of hatred still bursting into flame on a larger scale than I was dealing with.

They gave me a stiff lecture on loose cannons — or rifles — suggested I volunteered for one of the aid agencies, make a real commitment!

I thanked them and left.

Someone must, however, have made up a file after all. It resurfaced later, some years later, to impinge on my life.

8b

HE MOVES THROUGH the English air with an ease, fluidity, borne of power, the quiet resolution of a sheathed knife.

He need no longer check his shadow in the pallid light. He can float in the drift of other men, demobbed, neutered, winding themselves down or up to the tedium of work and domesticity.

Despite his ease he is bulked with pent aggression, disengaged. He outruns the dog, who is aging now, sprawls to await it, its soft licks, its eagerness, shuddering.

He feels flabby, immersed in a warm quotidian. Needs to regain the tensile alertness, the overstretch.

He wheels out his pre-war Raleigh, strips it down, cleans and greases the chain, bottom bracket, hubs, buffs the wheel rims, wire-brushes the spokes, pumps the tyres, retapes the bars.

He is calmed by the ticking of the wheels as they spin in the air, the balance of the bike as he pushes it, two fingers on the saddle. He mounts it, sprints up and down the road, turning tightly against the brakes, leaning over the bars.

He returns to the house, fills his water bottle, slings on his musette.

Now he can open up, push himself, pump his legs, chest, working through the gears. The hedges are blurring, flickering in his peripheral vision. He is losing himself, losing the inessentials of his soul.

Next morning finds him, still heavy, mounting the bike, warming his legs, then pushing against a stiffening headwind, out of the saddle for a final spurt, turning, almost coasting home, a cooling drizzle sopping his jersey.

After a bath and breakfast he finds an Ordnance Survey map, carefully measures a ten-mile course of varied gradients, clamps his stopwatch to the handlebars.

Now each day he is out, morning and evening, pacing himself over the course against the watch, shaving off minutes, then seconds in each one-man trial.

He compiles a log — times, conditions, wind speed, traffic — charts a graph of his prowess, pushing himself until the graph describes a plateau.

It has become a private agon, this daily descent into the limits of his being, the constraints more mental than physical, the tempering of his soul.

But an agon has to be antagonistic. The self can only be asserted against the push of others, the jostle of opponency.

He decides to make contact with his pre-war club, if it

still exists, institute one if it doesn't, found a company of sporting gods, mutual adversaries.

The amalgamation of several war-depleted clubs into one takes place, partly by his chivvying, his drive. They train together, club together, contact other renascent clubs, organise a calendar of club runs and races, a return to the tempo of pre-war life.

The evening before a race would see him poring over the Ordnance Survey map, visualizing the course, calculating the gradients from the contours, working out when to press his advantage, jump off from the bunch, launch a lone break up the climb. When to expect to be caught. When to pull his trick with the comb before jumping again, up to the summit.

After a solid night's sleep — the sleep of confidence — he rises early, makes his last-minute checks of his bike, spares, provisions, sets off to cycle to the start. He arrives at the check-in with his legs and heart warmed, tuned.

His usual tactic is to sit in with the bunch, who are idling, cantering, still warming up. He sits in, sometimes slipping to the back, conserving himself, reading the landscape, watching for the signs.

As the landmarks indicate the first climb ahead, he

tightens his toe-straps, fusing himself with the bike, a single animal. Works his way to the head of the field, suddenly launches himself, dropping the gears, spinning the pedals until the gradient begins to bite and he feels his legs fully engaged.

After a comfortable gap he eases, looks back, allows himself to be caught by a few front-runners, maintains his pace. As he feels the gradient lessen, he pulls out his comb, sits up off the bars, combs his hair.

Comb back in his jersey pocket, its psychological work done, he drops to the bars, head low, surges ahead once more, this time to the summit, over without a backward glance, shifting the gears up, launching into the descent to hold his advantage long enough to neutralize his inability over the flat.

On a good day, on the right course, the finish not too far from the last hill, he maintains his lead, maybe increasing it with the adrenalin of leading, pulls out the comb again just before the line, his slicked-back hair distracting from the grimed sweat-lines of his earlier exertion, building the legend of the effortless win, super-cool insouciance.

8c

I REALIZED AFTER TWO or three days of inactivity at home that my knee was stiffening up, but had given me no trouble all the time I was pedalling across the Continent. I decided to keep up the therapy, get back into the saddle, maybe meet up with whoever was left from the pre-war club.

There were a few, veterans by now, but several demobs had been encouraged to join—enough for a decent club run on a Sunday morning, though nothing competitive as yet.

I kept the tourer for training, got out my treasured racer, put together on a second-hand Bates frame just before the war, stripped and cleaned it. I would have liked some new tyres, but they were still impossible to come by. I patched and pumped the old ones and began some light training through the country lanes.

On a responsive bike, without the weight of panniers and sidecar, I was flying—the exhilaration of being one with a mechanically-perfect machine, responding to my touch on the bars, each jolt of the road through the wheels enhancing the sensation of control.

The countryside reeled past me as I stretched my legs and lungs. All the burdens and abrasions of *ticking* the last few years fell away.

I was up early the next morning, stuffed my musette with sandwiches and headed for Box Hill, try my legs out on a climb.

I could feel my knee grind a little when honking — out of the saddle, treading the pedals — but otherwise it held up fairly well. I nearly came off on my first descent, on a sharp bend I had forgotten, but after several climbs, my body and nerves were attuned, I was now part of the bike, no longer had to think. As in the war, I was now living a purely physical existence, literally *existing*, living outside myself, watching, interested. An experience I was to find becoming more frequent in later life, and increasingly corrosive. But at the time I thought little of it, concentrated on my fitness, on regaining my speed as a climber.

It's true that one does, after reaching a certain standard, need the stimulus of competition. So once we had recruited a few more young cyclists, I organised a return to the time-trialling meetings of pre-war days. I was able to work out several courses which incorporated stiff climbs, although hardly real hills, still less mountains. Nonetheless, I felt they gave me an unfair advantage, so I was careful to alternate them with flat courses, on which I was still disappointingly slow.

This was long before the days of drag-strip courses,

where the slipstream of motor traffic, lorries especially, pulls up your speed—there just wasn't that much traffic, even on arterial roads, in the early evening or weekends. So we were all achieving respectable times over ten and twenty-five mile courses. Soon, we all felt the need to compete against fresh blood, other clubs.

Our approach to the sport had changed, partly as a result of the war. Sadly the sport itself hadn't. When Stallard organised mass-start racing again in '42, he was expelled from the National Cyclists' Union, who still, along with the Road Time Trials Council, proscribed them.

Such was the strength of the NCU's propaganda—the fear of motorists' wrath and police action—that to begin with, a group of us organised illicit races, working out a course on the quietest back roads we could find, with an unobtrusive finish line—a string laid across the road at the last minute. But we were too inhibited to concentrate on racing—at the sign of approaching traffic we slowed down, pretending to be on a club run. Eventually we returned to time trialling, the 'English sport'.

But it wasn't enough. Those of us who had been overseas had developed an interest in proper, continental-style racing. We followed avidly the one-day classics—Paris-Nice, Paris-Roubaix—and the Tours—the Giro d'Italia, Tour of Flanders. Above all, the Tour de France, which had just resumed in '47.

Several of the younger members had learnt French,

enough to read the sports reports in the French papers. We would gather in the clubhouse and listen as Bob Ashton or Ken Beesley falteringly translated aloud from the latest, week-old copy of *L'Equipe*.

Coppi was a hero to most of us, but to me especially.

We had ambivalent feelings about the Italians after the war — we felt that they had been seduced by Germany, were not solidly Fascist, and most of them changed sides anyway. But Coppi was beyond these considerations. He was not an Italian, but a Roman god, after winning the Giro in '46, and becoming an honorary Frenchman from '49 when he took the yellow jersey in his first Tour — a lead of 20 minutes on the col Izoard.

Coppi — the 'heron'. Ungainly off the bike, but on it he flew, up the mountains and away.

He was ahead in other ways too, the first to use a double chainwheel.

Even rear dérailleur mechs were long proscribed in the Tour, as making things too easy for the riders, too reliant on mechanics. But eventually they had to relent and allow them in the Tour of '37.

As every rider, every team, had them, no one had an advantage. They just made life easier, especially in the mountains. Prior to that, rear wheels had just two free-wheels, either side of the hub. The rider had to get off at the start of a climb, take off his rear wheel, turn it round. And when he reached the summit, turn it back again.

It was not unknown for riders who knew the climb to jump off when the gradient appeared to indicate a descent, pretend to change their wheel round, then pedal off, leaving other riders who had followed suit and actually turned theirs round stuck in an impossibly high gear when the gradient changed and the climb began again.

Tactics. Another name for cheating, in our view, but the Tour was war, no holds barred, any psychological advantage taken.

The comb trick, for example, belonged to a Swiss rider called Koblet—a natural mountains man, obviously, who rode the Tour in the early Fifties. It was not a stroke I would have thought of or been capable of pulling. I wish I had been.

I do have to admit that the double chainwheel (which virtually doubles the number of gears) did give me a psychological advantage for a season or two, having been able to obtain one from France through a contact of my father's. Once I had worked out the gear ratios and practised changing smoothly, it gave me an edge even before the time trial as well as during it.

I used that advantage to the full while I had it. I became better on the flat and unassailable on climbs.

The anti-race propaganda of the NCU turned out to be just that—police support in fact was good, motorists didn't much object. We, along with many clubs, abandoned the Union and affiliated to the British League of Racing Cyclists, founded by Stallard, which organised massed-start races for both amateurs and professionals.

I built up my collection of Ordnance Survey maps to study the contours and gradients of each course — a benefit of my map-reading experience during the war. I was able to pinpoint where to attack, where to hold back, where to jump, ideally on a bend followed by a steep climb which, if late enough in the course, would give me a lead I could hold onto to the finish. Which didn't happen often.

I was by this time working as a postman. Hardly a vocation in my father's eyes, but it allowed me to train in the afternoons, ride the evening time trials of neighbouring clubs, compete on Sundays. And the heavy delivery bike was training in itself. That way my knee never had time to stiffen.

Weekends during the season I would sometimes ride a hundred miles or so on the Saturday afternoon to a distant race, staying overnight in a B&B, ride the race on Sunday morning, cycle home in time for Monday's delivery. We thought nothing of it at the time; there was little alternative if you wanted to race. And I did.

In part, it was a vocation, perhaps. In part it was a link with my past, a way of converting the war into a hiatus, a way to stop it destroying me, as it destroyed others, sunk into a restless apathy.

But all that happens to you, happens, changes the contours of your life.

9a

MCKUEN WALKED, PUSHING his bike, to the starting line, limping heavily, leaning on the saddle.

He mounted, wincing visibly, flipping the pedal over to engage the toe clip, waited for the flag, breathing evenly, consciously, blinkering his mind.

He had dropped eighteen minutes to the leaders in the previous day's time trial — a flat course, one-way against a vindictive headwind. He knew he had to make up the deficiency and add a good five minutes to put him in with a chance.

The flag swooped down. He pushed himself off, engaged the other toe clip and set off in the middle of the bunch. There were twelve kilometres of the stage before they would begin the incline of the first climb, a short descent on a hairpin bend, and the long steepening climb to the finish. He has measured it, paced it in his mind from the maps, the night before.

He worked his way to the back of the bunch, holding on, being towed for six or so kilometres, then allowing himself to be dropped as they began the surge, the jockeying for positions ready for the first break of the stage. He kept them in view, adjusting his pace to keep the distance constant. They had seen him struggling, noticed his limp to the start, his straggling at the back. Now they had no thought of him. The stage had started in earnest.

Already the overall leader, the Belgian, is in trouble, the pain on his face reflecting the forced pace. But it's still early in the race for such suffering. In fact, it wasn't his legs or lungs, but unseen abrasion. The fine sand that had been rubbed into the chamois insert of his shorts in the drying room at dead of night had now worked through to the surface, drawn by his sweat, corroding into his flesh, eroding his spirit.

Two of his team *domestiques* work their way through the bunch to flank him, tow him out off the front to break away so he can, clear of the jostle, get out of the saddle, tread his way on his biggest gear, build up enough of a lead to freewheel, pour the contents of his water bottle into the back of his shorts in a futile attempt to wash away the grit.

By now the pack were on to them, sweeping round, swallowing them in its swarm, finally spitting the Belgian from the rear as he freewheels to the verge, awaiting the wagon.

There were only three kilometres before the climb begins; the non-climbers — the flat men — need to build a lead now if they were to survive.

The first attack is Dutch, their team leader jumping

away as the team block and control the bunch. But the pace is being forced. After a kilometre the breakaway is reeled in, broken-winded, to rest in the bunch steadying himself for the slog of the incline.

Already the gradient is changing, stiffening.

Five kilometres up, the bunch has split, splintered, the climbers bobbing to the front, leaving the flatmen, the detritus, to drift back, fighting gravity, fighting inertia.

McKuen has been shadowing, slowly decreasing his distance from the bunch. Now he begins his surge, bearing down on the demoralized rump of the pantheon, coming from nowhere. He reaches down, tightens each toe strap in turn, ducks his head, steadies his air intake, swerves round the loosely packed bunch, flicking through the gears as the gradient bites.

Now he's picking off the avant-garde one by one, not looking round as he spins past, spokes flashing in the sun, resorting at times to sideways tacking but still in the saddle, power to spare.

Almost at the first summit he takes the two leaders, pulling as an ad hoc team, an uneasy alliance of convenience which does them no good. As he drops them, McKuen straightens, pulls a banana from his jersey, unpeels it two-handed, eats, tosses the skin away, drops to the bars, surges over the summit, changing up the gears for the hairpin descent, down again for the final long climb.

This is the testing of every climber — the long haul up, alone, struggling to hold the lead, unable to gauge the progress of the riders below, both gravity and doubt dragging, pulling, probing the sinews of the soul.

But McKuen has spent time in hell, he's acclimatized. His mind shuts down, idles, as he focuses on his wheel and the metres of road, alert for every flint, every thorn.

Towards the peak is a gaggle of spectators lining the outer verge of the road, clustering the route. As he tacks across the road a stick shoots out with a sponge impaled. He takes the sponge, douses his face and neck, avoiding his chest, trickling it down his back.

As he throws away the sponge, a water bottle is thrust from the crowd. This he rejects — a gut warning that proves correct. The next rider up accepts, cramping almost immediately from the salt in the water.

Now the non-partisan and pro-English elements of the crowd are encroaching on the road to urge him on, patting his back, pushing, propelling him physically and mentally. One shouts his name, pushing a packet into his rear pocket as he pats him on the back.

McKuen is aware of the packet, cool, burning his back. But he's concentrating again on his wheel, watching for the grit, tacks, sticks poked at his spokes. He's almost there.

Still he doesn't look behind him. Every last ounce of strength goes into the final spurt, out of the saddle now, rolling from side to side, treading the altitude-light air, the tape shimmering, receding, on the road ahead.

But there, it's beneath his wheel now, beneath his pedal, it's in his past, he's there, gasping, toppling with the bike into the arms of the supporting crowd.

He sits on the grass, freed from the bike, allowing the minutes to tick past as he awaits the first of the field, his dusted face bronzed by the late flooding light.

Sixteen minutes pass, seventeen, ten, twenty, thirty, thirty-seven seconds. Every second will be hoarded to offset the losses on the next stage. An even, mostly flat stage.

He'll be in the pantheon, resting, watchful, aware of the others watching him, his every move, every feint.

But that's a day away.

He sits forward, apparently massaging the small of his back as riders sputter across the line.

After the meal and makeshift shower, McKuen took his bike from the van, greased the chain and pedal bearings, adjusted the brake blocks. It was late, quiet, the rest of the team in the hostel. He eased off the front tyre, checked the inner tube for slow punctures, took the packet from his kit bag, carefully separated the greaseproof sheets, tucked them into the tyre, spreading them round the circumference, levered the tyre back on with his thumbs, pumped the tyres hard.

He slept the night with his bike next to his bed.

The next day was cloudy, occasional drizzle slicking the road. His aim was merely to stay with the bunch, finish the stage, holding as much of his lead as he could, knowing it would be whittled down by the sprinters.

Once his lead was gone, he was under orders to feign injury or crash, retire from the race. He was buggered if he was going to do that. He was aiming to finish, as *lanterne rouge* if necessary.

A ribbon, a glint of medal, dangled in the edge of his vision. But this was his present, maybe his future; another sphere of action, a new arena. Charley Holland, Bill Burl had ridden the Tour de France in '37, held creditable placings, were respected as *Anglais sportifs*, determined underdogs. There was room for others. He felt at home here, in the Alps, on Olympus.

But. There was the weather. The rain on the road. The risk of puncture. If he punctured in his front tyre he was finished. He couldn't risk a wheel change, still less help in mending the puncture.

With luck, the greaseproof paper would be enough to deflect any flint.

The first ten kilometres were neutralized, no points given for attacking, so the whole field set off, caped, with a relaxed carnival atmosphere despite the drizzle, just cameraderie and the feel of the bikes beneath them, the waves of the crowd.

The drizzle intensified into a hard rain, but with a lightening of the sky in the distance. As the neutralized section ended, the teams began to form, the water-carriers grouping round the leaders, pushing up the pace as the feints and attacks started, to test, probe the strength and resolve of the rivals.

McKuen, in his leader's sash, was exempt from domestic duties, free to find his position toward the rear of the bunch, mechanise his mind, maintain the rhythm he needed to hold on, half coasting in the slipstream.

But the exertions of yesterday's climb have not yet worked off, his legs are still heavy, the rhythm won't come. He finds himself slipping toward the back as the pace is whipped up from the front by the early attacks.

They're rolling through undulating roads, lazy bends, a few hedgerows hemming in the riders. He's struggling now, continually dropped, clawing his way back.

Rounding a bend, the bunch surge, leaving him trailing, winded. As he corners he sees a movement just in vision, a rock rolling toward his front wheel. He brakes and swerves to protect his rim, his bike rearing and skidding, the rock catching his chainwheel, toppling him.

He lies in the hedgerow, stunned at first, grateful for the respite. Then starts calculating the possibilities. Simple anti-British feeling? An enforcer? Or just the usual partisan spectator? He decides to play safe.

The van picks him up. His race is over for the day. He sits in the van as the hedgerows flicker past, carefully slitting the side of the front tyre, puncturing the inner tube, listening for the hiss.

In the hotel he takes the tyre half off, retrieves the papers, counting the sheets, putting the tyre back on, the puncture unrepaired. The chainwheel is buckled; they have no spares. He will need to use the one spare bike.

Up in the bedroom, he spreads the sheets across his bed, forming a square, takes his Kodak from his kit bag, photographs the square several times, folds the papers again, takes them to the stables where the bikes are stored for the night, works them into the front tyre of the spare bike, making a show of checking the rest of the bike, then rejoins the team for supper.

The next day's stage — the final — was the crucial stage for McKuen. He woke early, apprehensive, cuts on his legs still stinging, knee aching.

They breakfasted on muesli, toast, horse-meat risotto, stocked up on dried fruit, made their way to the start.

After a short neutralized section, the course would

swing toward the border in a long looping arc, with three second-category climbs, before crossing back to the west for a finish in full view of the eastern sector, so the border would, in the spectators' experience of the race, disappear. A Peace Race. The power of sport to rise above politics, unite people in an idealistic pursuit.

As the field moved off, McKuen began to relax; soothed by the rhythm, his legs no longer ached, his mind cleared, he had only to pedal.

The sky was overcast but the air was warm, heavy with the scent of scythed meadows. Even in the neutralized opening the pace was high, every rider determined to make his mark on the last stage.

They swung into the approach to the border, slowed into a double file, counted through the barrier, regrouped for the last kilometre of the neutralized section. Then the attacks began.

McKuen had placed himself well, tucked into the outer ring of the bunch, allowing riders to jump off the centre without being blocked by their *domestiques*. He had studied the maps, calculated exactly where to go clear for the first climb.

He pulled some raisins from his jersey pocket, chewed them in rhythm with his cadence. He could feel the pull of the gradient, began to read the landmarks.

The climb would begin immediately after a right-hand bend, hidden by the hedgerow. He ducked his head, appearing to be checking his front wheel, so he could drop gear surreptitiously, spin his way round the bend, then tread and push ahead.

It worked. The confusion, the hasty attempts to find a gear while stuck in a high, left the field floundering, gave McKuen vital seconds to distance himself, settle his rhythm, settle his mind.

He pushed back in the saddle, arms pulling the bars, legs punching.

He had to tack for half a kilometre, glancing over his shoulder at the shredded field strung out along the road. Then the gradient eased.

He came out of the saddle for a few minutes to consolidate his lead, then dropped back down, refound his rhythm, pulled steadily up the final climb.

There were spectators knotted around either side of the summit, some with bikes. He scanned them, but had no idea of who to look for. But as he crested the col he could see the rock ahead to his right, half-hidden in the grass. He swerved across, hit the rock at an angle to topple him into the grass, skidded down the slope with the bike anchored to his feet.

Still winded, he reached and released the toe straps, disentangled the bike, got to his feet. The front wheel was nicely buckled.

He began to move it back and forth. One of the spectators with a bike pushed forward, pulling his own front wheel off, thrusting it forward.

McKuen took it, hoping this was the one, released his wheel from the fork drop-outs, slotted in the stranger's.

The man stood holding his own bike forks up, the buckled wheel between his legs. McKuen nodded his thanks, relief.

As he mounted, the first of his rivals thundered over the summit, freewheeling now. McKuen pushed himself off, spinning manically until he could find his biggest gear, began punching down on the pedals, almost bounding clear of the road as the descent dipped away.

He caught the rider, fastened onto his wheel. But there was nothing to be gained from slipstreaming on a descent, so he resumed pedalling, dropped the rider, who was startled to see someone not freewheeling, hurtled round the twists of the descent.

There was still another climb later. But nothing now mattered. They would be stripping his tyre by now, slipping out the numbered sheets, and his hand-written postscript.

He had added to his lead by his crazed descent, although he had no way of measuring it. His momentum carried him well on the way to the final climb.

He was relaxed now, his eye on the strange-patterned tyre, his legs pumping methodically, adjusting automatically to the variations in the gradient. He was out on his own, clear and free.

He was still by himself as he swung back across the border on the finishing straight, though his lead had been reduced by a trio of riders working together. He knew anyway that it wouldn't be enough to give him an overall win. But it no longer mattered, was not the objective.

He barely acknowledged the crowd round the finish, continued riding to wind down his legs, let his pulse slow.

He was quiet throughout the journey home, sitting in the van with the bikes rather than in the car with the team.

On the ferry he stood at the stern, wakeful as the others slept on the decks. He kept his kit bag with him.

They split up at Dover. McKuen took the train into London, changing at Victoria to a bus that took him past the Whitehall address to which he'd been instructed to walk from the stop beyond.

He was exercised, on the bus, by the pleasant dilemma of his report. Should he inform his control that he had tipped off his contacts? A double, or a triple cross?

He decided in a moment's exhilaration to decide it by the toss of a coin. He reached into his pocket for a half-crown, enjoying the piquancy of the pun.

9b

IT'S TRUE THERE was a race, through Belgium, France and Germany, an attempt to revive the Socialist Peace Rides of the twenties, organised by the Sports For Peace League.

A few of us, mostly ex-Forces, had been over to France for a couple of summers running, signing up for local races as we encountered them, picking up enough between us in *primes* to cover our food and lodging, the aim being to gain enough experience to be taken on by a professional team. That didn't happen. But when this — strictly amateur — race was organised, I was invited to join the team. Only me, which I thought odd at the time. Several of the others were better all-round riders than me. I just assumed they wanted a climber, although my experience of real mountain riding was nil. Box Hill is not *flint* the col Izoard, after all.

Then I discovered the reason for my inclusion.

I had a telephone call 'inviting' me to attend a briefing in Aldershot.

I presented myself before a panel of two in a Nissen hut well away from the barracks. A little chat about my war record, my transition to civilian life, family, 'spouse possibilities', values. Followed by mention of a report — which lay on the desk — filed by the ICC, concerning my 'postwar adventures' and the dropped charges. Charges which could, I was given to understand, be reactivated. No mention, by the way, of the medal.

I was simply to receive a report and carry it home. I was not an agent, still less a spy. I was no more than a *domestique*, a water-carrier. Literally, since the report was to be passed to me — on a mountain stage, it's true — in a water bottle.

I was in fact trailing, rather than leading, but still alone, behind the bunch, when it was passed to me.

We didn't have particular bikes allocated to us for the race. The team bikes, including two spares, were rotated, so we wouldn't necessarily have the same bike two days running. I was able, though, to insist on taking my own saddle which I could swap from bike to bike, using my knee as excuse.

We were, as usual in those days, as today, using tubs — tubular tyres with the inner tube sewn in and the whole carcass glued to the wheel rim with shellac. No way of secreting papers inside. I'm surprised that as a novelist he didn't check that.

I rolled up the report and slid it into the stem of my saddle.

Neither did we cross into the Russian-occupied zone.

The truth was more prosaic, although possibly more bizarre. The report in fact concerned American activity rather than Russian. But you can imagine the diplomatic embarrassment if it came out that we were spying on our allies, which is why normal channels were not risked.

I wasn't, of course, told this at the time.

Overall, our relative lack of experience of continental conditions told against us, and me in particular, even against other amateurs. But we acquitted ourselves well, engendered, we hoped, the spirit of sporting fraternity in the population at large. And my mission was accomplished without mishap.

Actually, I was quite pleased with my performance. I did take the lead in two mountain stages, winning one, and on the flat was able to keep in with the bunch without too much strain.

Incidentally, the term for the main bunch is *peloton*, not *pantheon*. He could at least get the terminology right.

On arrival in England, I retrieved my saddle, slung it into my kit bag, got the train home. Then slipped the saddle stem back into my own bike and pedalled over to Aldershot.

I banged the saddle stem on the desk, so the packet slid out, rolled across the blotter. And that was that. No report, no commendation, no explanation. Just told to carry on with my life.

Which wasn't as easy as it sounded.

I no longer knew what I wanted in life. I was still working as a postman, to my father's disappointment, while deciding what to do next. I had thought of moving to France again, join the ACBB — the Athletic Club Boulogne-Billancourt — which I had heard were ready to accept foreign riders; try to carve out a career as a professional. But I was no longer sure I would make the grade, or whether my knee would stand the rigours of an almost year-round season.

And besides, perhaps inevitably, and belatedly, I had met a woman.

I met her first on the boat home. I thought I had caught a glimpse of her among the crowd at the finish of the mountain stage, the one I had won. But I couldn't be sure.

It was the saddle, however, that she remarked on. I was carrying it sticking out of my kit bag on deck. She knew about the race, asked about the team, our placings, times. I had the feeling she'd been coached, but again it was a passing impression.

We had a cup of tea to celebrate our return to English waters, chatted. A ship-board romance of an hour and a half. I never expected to see her again.

A week later she telephoned me at home. How she found

the number I never knew; she hadn't even asked my name. I assumed she contacted the race organiser; I never asked. I felt almost superstitious about spoiling my luck.

She lived in Richmond. I arranged to go and see her, cycled over. A route that became familiar.

I would leave my bike at her house and we'd walk up Richmond Hill into the park, walk amongst the deer, sit amidst the bracken. The bracken's acrid scent awoke memories, hungers for both danger and comfort. Mostly we talked.

She had worked in the Treasury during the war, under Iris Murdoch, who was vaguely her boss. She had, or had had, strongish left-wing views, which she'd had to keep hidden. We discussed them at length.

I had never been politically minded, just had an instinctive feeling for justice and the underdog, which I'd acted on, of course, but which had never been theoretical. A lot of what she said made sense.

So did our closeness, equally untheoretical, although I sometimes felt she was rewarding me for agreeing with some opinion or other. But I wasn't going to analyse it. It just felt right.

The first time we made love was there in the bracken, a picnic rug over us, waterproof beneath. I kept thinking of the German girl with the dead baby, and bruised her with my frantic burrowing.

She seemed to understand, and later reject, the mixture of protectiveness and hate.

It was later, over the course of months of lovemaking, mostly in her house, in a small terrace at the bottom of the hill, that our relationship took shape, its contours gradually fixed.

Those contours bounded my life, death, and into them I relaxed into something approaching peace.

The ritual — for it became ritualistic — was unvarying and always new. I would begin on my knees as she sat on the bed, my head in her lap. I would catch the tang of bracken in my throat as I kissed her thighs. Impatiently she would beckon me up and I would swing astride her, my knee throbbing from the kneeling.

She would give a strange, feral little whimper when she came, and I could let go, freewheel into sleep.

Usually I would wake in minutes, kiss her lowered eyelids, and she would turn her back, nestle into me. I would close my eyes, seeking her out in the velvet dark and gaining entry, pierce some membrane between life and death. I would adjust then to the changed contours and together we would drift.

When I awoke, normally an hour or so later, she would be smoothing my hair, whispering *ma pauvre, ma pauvre*.

I never quite understood that.

But this was all a long time ago and, later, she left me.

10a

THE BACKYARDS OF south London reeled past the lowered window. McKuen slung his kit bag up into the luggage rack, sank into the seat, inhaling its scent of heated dust. He sat back and, to relieve his aching knee, put his feet up onto the opposite seat. As he settled, a woman entered the compartment from the corridor. Hastily he took his feet off the seat, stood up.

—Please. Be comfortable. I can sit here beside you. Your legs, they still ache?

—Clairvoyant or a lucky guess?

—I watched the race.

—You recognize me?

—But of course. You gave a good ride.

—Are you a cycling fan?

—Ah yes. Since I was a little girl I have loved them.

—You live on the Continent, then?

—Not now. My husband, he is English. We have married since before the war, I thank God. My family . . .

—They are still there?

—Mostly dead.

—I'm sorry.

—Your first statement. But not necessary. You did not kill them.

—The Germans? Have you forgiven them yet?

—It does not occur, it is not appropriate. The whole world convulses. How can you speak of forgiving except of individuals?

—You still hate them, then?

—It is the same. It makes no sense.

—Then concentrate your hatred, focus on one individual at a time. That's the way.

—It is how you have found it? You have experience?

—I was a sniper. During the war. It's how I worked. One German at a time.

—But it is now negative. Now we must look ahead, put it in the past, they say. It is years now.

—They are still going to stay dead. Your relatives.

She turned away, looking through the window, silent. Sunlight filtered through the hair over her shoulders. Sensing McKuen's gaze, she caught up her hair into an impromptu ponytail before shaking it out again.

McKuen spread his handkerchief on the opposite seat, put up one leg. He didn't find the silence oppressive.

He felt the train slowing, knew she would get out at the next station. He fumbled in his jacket pocket.

As she stood up, pulling on her gloves, he gave her a card.

—Look, if you ever want to talk to me . . .

—You are a doctor?

—No. My father. But he'll take a message.

She put the card into her clasp bag.

He opened the carriage door for her.

—*Au revoir, Madame.*

She put a gloved finger to her lips, stepped out onto the platform, walked quickly away.

McKuen crossed the compartment, took the seat next to the corridor and put up his leg again, partly for relief, partly to deter anyone from entering. He closed his eyes.

On arriving home he dumped his kit bag, changed into shorts, wheeled out his bike, set off for a training spin before dinner. They had heard rumours, on the Peace Race, of a possible Tour of Britain, strictly amateur but organised on professional, continental lines. He wanted to maintain his competition fitness, in case.

His life resumed its rhythm of work, training, time trials and club runs, occasional races, apart from trips to Old Compton Street to track down the continental sports papers. He hoped some of them might have covered the Peace Race. None mentioned it.

Neither was there any more news of a British tour.

He came home, soaked through, from a training run to find a note by the telephone. A lady had called, left no number but would call back later.

He recognized her voice, realizing as he did so that he didn't know her name.

—This is McKuen? So, your father, he took my message? You do not remember our meeting, perhaps.

—On the contrary. I just hadn't expected . . .

—From things you said, I believe you can help me. I think you understand me, understand dilemmas that face me. You will not refuse me?

—I never refuse a call for help.

She gave him an address in Guildford, with instructions to wait beyond the gates.

Next afternoon he set out on his usual route to Box Hill but turned off before Dorking, cut through Abinger Forest into Guildford. He found the road not far from the cathedral, sat on his bike outside the house, feeling conspicuous.

An upstairs curtain twitched, the front door opened. She came down the drive, called him in and up a side path through to the garden.

She unlocked a summerhouse. He hid his bike carefully under the camellias, followed her in.

They sat together on a swinging seat. The air, unstirred for weeks, was musty, soporific. As if still training, he switched off his mind, waiting for her move. She was gazing out into the garden. Finally she braced herself.

—My husband, he doesn't understand. He is, like you, English. But he has no experiences, nothing that will touch him. He tells me, I must put the past behind, look ahead, for life with him. I cannot do this.

—You are not ready for that.

—I think I never will be ready. But I must. Only, they are there, my family, calling to me, not to be forsaken. I cannot swim free. It is a problem of love — for my husband, for them.

—No, the problem is hate. You do not hate. You told me so. No forgiveness can come without hatred first.

—I have tried. One cannot hate a whole nation. It has not helped.

—Do you remember what I said on the train?

He stood up. By the door, in an elephant leg holder, stood some umbrellas. He strode over, picked one out, held it horizontal at shoulder height.

He went back to the seat, put his arm round her neck, held the umbrella to her shoulder, pointing it through the door.

—This is a rifle. Look along it, through the sight. Past the rockery, you make out a helmet. Keep your eye fixed on it, wait for it to move. Now. He's standing up, he's off his guard, he's feeling for a cigarette. It's maybe your only chance. Your finger's on the trigger. You're ready, ready to kill him? Aim at his chest. He's a sitting duck. When I say the word, pull the trigger. Now.

She stiffened, recoiled.

—Did you get him?

—I couldn't. I couldn't shoot.

—Why not?

—I cannot kill him.

—You must. You have to kill him. Or you have to forgive him. You have to decide, you have to choose. Whatever you choose will affect the rest of your life, the rest of his life. Whatever you choose you choose for everyone. Okay. He's still there, he's drawing on his cigarette. It's almost through. You have another thirty seconds. What's it going to be? Look through the sight. Now. Decide.

—No, I cannot.

—You have to shoot or not shoot.

—I cannot shoot.

—You have forgiven him.

—I suppose.

—And if you forgive one, you have to forgive the rest. And now you have to accept the you you've chosen to live with. You can't go back.

He lowered the umbrella, tossed it aside. His arm was still round her neck. He could feel her unstiffening, softening.

—Life is choice. War teaches you that. But so does life. You have to practise living with your decisions, accepting the changes. You understand?

She nodded imperceptibly. Maybe it was merely a tremble.

He leaned into her, kissed her neck. She turned her head away, but gripped his arm, clinging grimly.

He made the trip to Guildford his weekly training, taking in Box Hill en route, arriving at the house stiff from the chafing, and the anticipation. He would enter the garden from the back lane, wait in the summerhouse. She would bring a bottle of wine and a single glass, and they would sip in turn, or he would drink from the bottle, sitting at her feet.

His homeward ride was a form of interval training, riding in spurts, impelled by elation, dragged by fatigue, his knees and thighs aching, dulled.

Plans for the Tour of Britain had solidified and he had intensified his training, knowing his performance in the Peace Race would make him a contender for one of the teams. He had in fact been approached tentatively by two sponsors — a cereal company, and a hair cream manufacturer wanting to utilise his trick with the comb, their advertising slogan already prepared ('Groomed To The Finish'). Neither came to anything.

He began to make the trip to Guildford more frequently and to climb Box Hill on both legs of the journey.

No one knew of his liaisons, but he was becoming restive. He wanted to show her off, introduce her round, have her cheering him on at the finishing line.

He was tired of finishing second.

—You don't really love him. You can't.

—I can, of course. I do.

—You say you love me.

—I do love you.

—You can't love us both.

—But of course. How ridiculous you are. If a woman has a second child, you think she stops loving the first? You are absurd.

—That's maternal love. This is different.

—It is the same.

—Have you told him? About me? Us?

—How can I? It would hurt him.

—It shouldn't. We are free agents. We give love freely, we receive it freely, in good faith. Anything else demeans both giver and receiver. He has to accept that. I accept it.

—He is English.

—So am I.

—He is older.

McKuen stormed up Box Hill, out of the saddle, honking the last incline, almost blind, heart rasping, legs giving out. At the summit he allowed himself to fall from the bike, sprawled into the grass, letting it cool him as his pulse calmed.

The letter was waiting for him when he got home. An invitation to a selection race for BSA, who were mounting a team for the Tour of Britain. It was a week ahead.

He said nothing about it to anyone in the club; just increased his mileage in training, pushed the pace on the weekend club run.

Neither did he mention it in the summerhouse. He said very little at all, drinking his wine from the bottle while she cradled the glass. But his lovemaking was tender and she clung to him quietly.

He avoided Box Hill on the way home, wanting to keep himself fresh for the selection race.

It was held in the Midlands, through the villages around Birmingham. They were supplying the bikes, so he went up on the train. He booked into the hotel taken by the company. There were around thirty riders invited. The atmosphere was edgy, and most of them, including McKuen, turned in early.

They were taken by bus, after an early breakfast, to a small, disused aerodrome in the outskirts of the town, its

Nissen hut the HQ for the race, the runway serving for start and finish.

They lined up, to attention, McKuen thought, legs apart while they were measured for their bikes.

As they lined up for the race he felt unusually nervous. He put it down to having to prove himself *before* being allowed to race. But as they got underway he felt the anger building up. As soon as they were clear of the town he converted the anger to energy, a surge of aggression through his legs that sent him clear of the bunch. It was untactical. Yet it worked, catching the others unawares.

As the gap widened he determined to stay ahead as long as possible, at least make his mark on the race.

Even the selectors had been unprepared for such an early attack and had to accelerate past the bunch to keep him in sight. Their car was now behind him but he seemed oblivious, emptying his mind, concentrating on the yard of road ahead of his wheel.

The miles rolled beneath. He was maintaining, even increasing, his lead, gearing up and coming out of the saddle every so often. But the energy from the original burst of anger was dissipating, he could feel his legs tiring. It was only a matter of time before he was swallowed by the bunch, maybe dropped. There were no climbs to speak of, no way of regaining his advantage then.

The selectors' car was half a mile behind him, probably equidistant from him and the bunch. There was a sequence of sharp bends ahead. He accelerated away, rounded the first bend, leaned down, first freewheeling then pedalling slowly backwards, fingers skimming the chain. He located the split link, eased off the circlip with his thumbnail, started pedalling, spinning rather than pushing, cornering fast, leaning into the bend.

Then he was into the straight and began to push hard on the pedals.

He could see the car again when he ducked his head, and changed up, pushing harder. Now he could feel the chain grinding. He came out of the saddle again, treading the pedals, rolling the bike from side to side.

The grinding was worsening. He sat back onto the saddle, gripped the bars.

Then the link slipped and the chain parted and he was spinning, resistanceless, as the chain dropped away, snaking across the road.

He freewheeled to a standstill as the car drew up and stopped.

—What happened?

—Chain broke, I think.

The second passenger got out, ran across and retrieved the chain, holding it up in his handkerchief.

—Split link's come out.

—I thought it wasn't feeling too sweet.

—You'll have to wait for the van. It'll be right behind the bunch.

—How long have I got?

—Don't worry about finishing. I think you've proved yourself.

McKuen wheeled his bike to the verge as the first of the bunch swept past, registering his presence with surprise. He held up the chain, shrugged.

She was waiting for him in the summerhouse, wine chilled and opened.

—This looks expensive. Celebration?

—For you, yes.

—But not for you?

—I have told him, as you wished.

—How did he take it?

—Badly. Quietly, but I knew he was hurt.

—Stiff upper lip though?

—It is not grounds for flippancy.

—Flippant is the last thing I feel. Relieved, yes. He should be, too. Eventually he would have suspected something. You have been honest with him. He should be flattered, at least. And grateful.

—Grateful?

—Look, I never planned to take you away from him.

—So noble.

—Yes. Both of us. Because whatever love you give him

now is voluntary, freely given. You two, we two, meet on open ground, as free individuals. We make a fresh commitment each time we offer ourselves.

—You make it sound so easy.

—It can be. Besides, if you're not happy, why the wine? You could have told me to stay away. I have no hold over you.

—You think that? You understand me so ill?

He put his arms round her, feeling the tears soaking into his jersey. He told her, by way of amends, or distraction, of the selection race. He felt sufficiently confident now.

—Will you come and watch me race?

—Of course.

—Look, there's a Saturday time trial next week, on Chobham Common. Come to that.

He arrived early for the time trial, already warmed up from the ride over, but he couldn't sit still, so he left his kit bag and musette with the organiser and rode a part of the course, criss-crossing with a few other early arrivals.

There was no sign of her when they were given their numbers and the departures started. He was fifth off, ten minutes after the first. It was a relatively flat course, a simple out-and-back, the turn executed on an improvised lay-by of beaten earth. Apart from a capricious crosswind, there was little to stretch him other than the thought of whether she would turn up, and in time.

The jitters were affecting his concentration, his rhythm, and despite a last burst to the finish he had shaved only seconds off his personal best for the course. And still she wasn't there.

He squatted by the organiser's chair amid the bags and spare wheels and counted in the riders, but their times no longer mattered to him.

With three riders to finish, he saw her in the distance.

He mounted and rode to meet her, swung off the bike and held her, breathless, against him.

—I thought you weren't coming. How did you get here?

—Taxi, and a bus. Then I walked.

—In high heels?

—I said I was going shopping.

—Why not have told the truth? I thought we agreed, to be open?

—You agreed. Why rub in unnecessary hurt?

—Because it's more honest. How are your feet?

—Sore.

He laid down his bike, knelt, lifted her leg while she leaned on his shoulder, removed her shoe and massaged her foot. Then the other.

—Come on. There should be some tea brewing by now.

They went back to the mêlée around the finish. A kettle was heating on a primus, and biscuits and fruitcake being handed round.

Her appearance caused a ripple of interest. He introduced her as a friend, with a casual wave, took two mugs from his kit bag. She stood silent, shy, as they all compared times, discussed courses, equipment.

They sipped the milky tea. He also was silent now.

He walked her back into Chobham for her bus, one arm round her shoulder, the other pushing his bike. He felt complete.

—We should get a tandem. I mean it. My parents had one. You'd soon get the hang of it.

He saw her onto the bus, mounted and cycled behind it, pulled by its slipstream. Then as it turned off toward Woking he overtook, waved and pedalled away, aware he was showing off, and not caring.

On the club run next day there was banter about the mystery woman. He took it in good part, giving nothing away.

The letter arrived on a Wednesday, confirming his place in the BSA team, with a list of training dates in the run-up to the Tour. He cycled over to Guildford. She wasn't expecting him so he knocked at the back door.

She took him into the kitchen, closing the door to the hall.

—You would like tea? Like we had it at the race?

—Not particularly. No wine? It's a celebration.

She read the letter, handed it back, smiling.

—You must be pleased.

—My future's becoming clearer. All round.

She kissed him quickly, went into the cellar for the wine, passed it to him to open.

—We'll drink it in the summerhouse.

—Nothing's really changed, has it?

—It has. I came to you, didn't I?

Her attendance at local races became regular, her presence a looked-for part of each event, a welcome touch of glamour. She began to open up to his club mates, with still a trace of reserve. The ribbing had stopped, their relationship accepted, unresolved, unremarked.

Her presence, to him, became talismanic. If she failed to arrive by his 'off' he knew he would do badly. But she made the effort, sometimes both of them arriving before anyone else. They would lie on his cape, arm in arm, chatting or silent, wrapped in themselves.

Word had got round of his selection for the Tour, and like a gunslinger he was marked out, riders from rival clubs hoping for glory by besting his times. But he welcomed the challenge, the psychological testing. As long as she was there at the finish.

The first training ride came round. Again on the Birmingham course. He explained to her that he needed her there.

—Just a weekend.

—What excuse can I give?

—None. Just say you're going.

—I will try.

They travelled separately—she by train, he by bike—but stayed in the same hotel, on different floors. They breakfasted together, very early, she amused at the amount he was eating, working his way through the menu: porridge, kedgeree, bacon and egg, toast and marmalade.

He cycled to the aerodrome. The others were already there, accommodated in a boarding house nearby, in which he too had been billetted.

The coach had been looking for him.

His measurements were on record so his bike was waiting. He adjusted the saddle, then rode round to calm his nerves.

The course was the same as before but a little longer. After his breakaway in the selection race he felt he had nothing to prove, except to her and himself, but knew that this time he would have to finish.

In addition to the team, riders from local clubs had been invited, to simulate race conditions.

They rolled off at a leisurely pace, a small, elongated peloton. He sat well in the middle, content this time to mark time, wait for someone to lead out a break.

He had copied out a map of the route for her, suggested a few vantage points. But he didn't know exactly where she'd be.

After one or two feints, an attack was launched. The bunch didn't respond, allowing the attackers to tire themselves before swallowing them up, but it pushed up the pace, McKuen still ensconced.

They approached a double hairpin with a short descent, but the pace didn't slacken. As they negotiated the bends, a rear wheel skidded, nudging the front wheel behind. Half a dozen riders went down like dominoes.

McKuen swerved in time, skirted the tumbled riders, started to press on. He ducked and looked back. All but one were on their feet, remounting, pushing themselves off. But the one remaining rider, a team rider, was struggling to rise, badly winded, maybe worse.

McKuen had to go on, had to finish within two minutes of the bunch. But a team jersey is a team jersey. He swerved back, slid round.

—You alright?

—No real damage, I think. But my shoulder's shot up. You go on.

—Not a chance.

McKuen rolled for a few yards while his teammate remounted, checked his gears, called. He latched onto McKuen's rear wheel, McKuen sheltering him from the now stiffening headwind, trying to find a pace that wouldn't prove too fast for him but that would give them a chance of catching the bunch, who were well out of sight.

The road turned, so the wind now cut across and they altered formation, almost abreast.

—How's the shoulder?

—Holding up.

—We can do it.

McKuen pushed up the pace.

As they rounded a bend he saw her. She was wearing a scarf of larkspur blue over a white dress, but the scarf she had shawled round her head against the wind, so he wasn't at first sure it was her. As they past, she waved, but she seemed abstracted, withdrawn, the white sheath dress folding her in.

McKuen answered with an agonised nod as he gasped for breath, then ducked down and resumed pulling.

As they topped an incline they could see the bunch ahead, the team car yards behind. The bends and contours rendered them invisible to the car. McKuen turned.

—Hold my jersey till I tell you to let go.

Gripping the brake hoods he began pounding the pedals, all his force going into each downturn, his concentration on counteracting the bias from the drag on his jersey. He pushed up their speed, eating up the miles between them and the bunch.

They came round a bend and saw the tail of the bunch. McKuen shouted: Let go now, almost unseated as he was freed of the drag.

They caught the bunch with a mile to the finish, the car moving aside to allow them to join. They tucked in and held on as long as they could, McKuen straining, his knee grating, the other riding one-handed, his other arm now behind him in his jersey pocket.

They fell behind again, but crossed the line within the limit to take the same time as the bunch.

The team car door opened and the team manager climbed out, clipboard tucked officer-like under his arm. He approached McKuen.

—I saw what you did.

McKuen blanched. Had he seen the tow after all?

—A fine piece of riding. Unselfish. We weren't too sure after your solo effort last time. We needn't have worried. You're a team rider alright.

McKuen changed with the team and wheeled out his own bike.

— There's a bus laid on to the boarding house.

— Thanks but I'm staying in town.

— There's a team meeting after supper.

— I'll bunk off this one. Make my excuses, will you?

— Do my best.

— Rest that shoulder.

She was waiting in the hotel dining room, in a floral dress of varied greens.

— Well?

— You didn't win?

— This wasn't about winning.

— Still, what you did was brave.

— Hardly that.

She bent over the menu, the table lamp shadowing the contours of her face.

— You seem far away.

— I am here.

— Wishing you weren't? Look, forget him for at least the time we're here.

— It is not so easy.

— Later, you'll forget him, I promise. First, we'll eat.

— Everything on the menu again?

— We'll see what's on the menu.

He saw her to the train next morning, returned for his bike for the long trek home.

Training rides were arranged for fortnightly intervals until the month before the Tour.

She didn't come to the next, but still turned up for the local time trials, and a club picnic.

He didn't show well in the club events, aware that he was pacing himself for the Tour, doing as much and no more than necessary in training, too. But that was understood, approved. And in the training sessions, the team had now bonded, were riding cohesively. Although not the leader, he had the go-ahead to attack when he saw the chance, break away on his own if he felt he could sustain it. But would buckle down to pace or block when he had to.

The tension was beginning to build and he was responding. He felt good, confident.

So the letter, when it came, caught him off guard.

Dear Mr. McKuen,

We have been very impressed by your performance to date; by your prowess and speed, by your determination, and your unselfish devotion to the team spirit.
As you are no doubt aware, this is what we hope will

be the inaugural event for a regular, perhaps annual, Tour of Britain. With this in mind, we naturally have to set ourselves the highest standards in both sport and ethics, knowing the press and public will be taking a keen interest.

Therefore, in the interests of attracting future sponsorship, we have, reluctantly, to deny ourselves your abilities.

We regret the disappointment this is sure to cause you, and wish you every success in your future endeavours.

Sincerely,

He put the letter back into its envelope, stuffed it into his kit bag.

He pulled it out, handed it to her wordlessly.

— I don't understand.

— Word gets round.

— Only your friends know. It is him. It must be him.

— I thought he had no interest in cycling.

— He knows many people, in many places.

— Is he so petty?

— He doesn't see things as you do.

— Maybe he needs to be shown.

10b

Isabelle wasn't married; she was a widow, although not, as it happened, a war widow.

The idea of the affair with a married woman I suspect was based on Fausto Coppi's, probably for some novelistic play on his Christian name.

And the first Tour of Britain, which later became the Milk Race, was in 1955, years after the Peace Race. And years, too, after I had given up any ambition to become a professional cyclist. My knee, I acknowledged, wouldn't have stood up to it for a start. And I felt it time to settle down. Isabelle and I were developing something deeper, I felt, something lasting.

I applied for a transfer in the Post Office to counter clerk, sat the Civil Service Commission Clerical Grade exam, re-signed the Official Secrets Act, and started a nine-to-seven working week. I kept up the Sunday club runs and evening time trials, balancing my till and scooting off to make a late 'off' at seven-thirty.

I settled into the weekly routine, and, oddly for someone of my age perhaps, found it soothing, like finding your rhythm over a fifty-mile ride. And with no more early mornings, I could see more of Isabelle in the evenings. *Larkspur*

I'd cycle over to Richmond, lock up my bike on her railings, and we'd walk along the river. Or we'd go to the cinema, maybe twice a week. We used to discuss the films at length, sometimes heatedly, as we did other topics. She appeared to have strong opinions, but I could never be sure what they were. She seemed inconsistent. I sometimes had the feeling she was merely playing Devil's advocate; almost as if sounding me out.

I remember we'd once been to see a film called *Shadow of the Rope*, one of those English B-movies of the time, involving a girl who falls in love with a man condemned to death for the murder of her brother.

She questioned me almost forensically: did I believe the State had the right to take a life for a life? Did I think forgiveness possible? Did I believe in redemption by love?

As to the first, she had once declared herself in favour of the execution of collaborators; now she seemed to be arguing the opposite.

As to love, she thought forgiveness should be limitless, otherwise it wasn't love.

I found reassurance in that. I wasn't sure how much of my past she knew about, how much I had told her after we first met.

So, although I never felt entirely clear about where I

stood in her estimation, I did think we were building a foundation for the future.

Then she disappeared.

I went to the house as usual—she was out, and the house felt hollow. I asked her neighbours, whom I'd never met. They could tell me nothing, hardly knew her. It turned out she had only moved in just before, or maybe after, meeting me.

I heard nothing from her.

If she'd broken with me, I could have accepted it, in time. But as it stood, not knowing anything of her motives, feelings, whereabouts, I was emotionally back in No-Man's Land; not able to progress or retreat, every attempt to move on increasing the confusion, the anger, the . . . stasis.

Local silence and the smoke in your throat . . .

I made a conscious effort to forget her, as I had Swain. But, as with him, I found she was always there, turning every casual affair into a *ménage à trois*.

Look, none of this is in the novel. It's all so dry, so cold. I've spent my life hiding my emotions—you have to, to survive—hidden even from my self. There are feelings we don't even understand ourselves. That's what we look to novelists for.

Okay, he's researched the cycling, the fictionalization I expect, reality is mostly humdrum, but emotion, motivation . . .

If you're going to tamper with a man's life, at least provide some insight. Not this absurd existential anti-hero.

Maybe it's as well. Better dryness than melodrama. At least my emotional terrain remains intact. It would likely have been travestied had he entered it.

11a

Mckuen alighted lightly from the train, strode to the barrier, shouldered his way through the station.

He found the door from memory. It had evidently been repainted since, but still evinced a decade's shabbiness. He pushed it open, knocked on the inner door.

—Come.

He didn't think it was the same man, but it might have been. He showed no surprise at McKuen's entrance.

—What can we do for you?

—It's rather the other way round.

—*Sir.*

—I'm civilian. Sir.

—Of course. So what can you do for us? *Mr . . .?*

—McKuen. The arms raid, in Aldershot.

—How do you know about that?

—I read the papers. I understand the weaponry included Enfield Mk. 4s. They're sniper rifles.

—You read remarkably well-informed newspapers, Mr. McKuen.

—*The Farnborough Gazette*. Local.

—Which brings you, I trust, to your point?

—It seemed a well-organised raid. They knew what they wanted. If they've taken Enfield 4s, they must intend to use them. The only way to defeat a sniper is to deploy a sniper.

—And you're volunteering?

—Sir.

—Very public-spirited, Mr. McKuen. But you realize, of course, the Army *has* snipers?

—I get the impression this will need to be handled without involving the Army. Am I right?

—You're very astute, McKuen. But that hardly makes it a civilian concern.

—I've worked for you before. I'm sure there'll be a file.

—I'm sure there will. Let me consult it and I'll let you know.

—Sir.

—Right. I'll be in touch. Close the door after you, would you? . . . *Quietly*, next time.

The scrambled message was taken down by his father two days later.

He made the same journey, pushed open the doors, sat down at the desk. His file was on the blotter.

—Thank you for coming in, McKuen. As you see, we've studied your file. Bit of a wild card, aren't you?

—Isn't that why you used me? Plus the fact that I was expendable. Well, I'm still expendable. Besides, it's wild cards you need. Do you think these people will abide by Queen's Regulations?

—You do realize we are unable to arm you? Binoculars and a field telephone will be your only tools. You'll be purely advisory, reconnoitring possible sniper hides, suggesting their tactics, targets. You'll point out their position and stand back. Understood?

—Sir.

—Do any rambling?

—No. Cycling. *Walking*, for God's sake?

—Too conspicuous. Pose as a twitcher. Assuming they're rural campaigns.

—If they're urban?

—Intelligence suggests they won't be. That's what the bombs were for. Right. Buy yourself shorts, boots, rucksack. Don't forget the receipts. Tickets will be posted. Clear?

—Sir.

§

The mist thickened, finally resolved into rain, curtailing visibility to fifty yards.

McKuen found a hollow in the turf, stretched his cape over two sticks, settled himself in. He pulled the primus from his rucksack, got a brew going. Doubtless the squad would be doing the same, but in the dry back of a lorry. But he relaxed, focusing his hearing, tuning out the drip and drizzle.

As he sipped the tea he took out his bird identification book, began leafing through, noting the possible spottings. He was enjoying this.

The clouds began to clear, the sun broke through. He pulled the rucksack open, cranked the field telephone, leaned over to shield the mouthpiece.

—Jacksnipe. I'm moving off now, northeasterly.

He tied the cape round his waist, hoisted the rucksack.

As he walked, he ostentatiously swept the sky with his binoculars, then consulted the bird book. Then dropped to his knees to pan along the hedgerows.

Suddenly he stopped, panned back. There was a gap in the nettles along the hedge, where they had possibly been flattened. He could just detect a fleck of white. He focused on it for several minutes, slowing his breathing. No sign of movement.

He tacked across to it unhurriedly.

A declivity in the grass and nettles about the size of a torso, indentations in the earth. And the corner of a cigarette packet crushed into the hedge. He pulled it out. It was sodden, pulpy, evidently been there overnight at least. He tossed it aside.

He followed the hedgerow, looking for birds' nests, making his way toward a cover of hawthorn.

He held the bird book in one hand, blundered into the trees.

No sign of anyone, which is as he had expected. Trees were too obvious a hide. He continued along the hedgerow, every so often sweeping back to the trees, up into the sky with the binoculars, fixing on a skylark in his mind's eye, spiralling up. Then dropped to his knees in a patch of scrub, surveyed the curve of the hedge beyond.

Nothing showed. Nor in the undulating turf lying back from the hedge. Yet he felt the old tingle in his spine. Somehow he knew that was the placement. He cranked the telephone.

—Jacksnipe. Slight incline fifty to seventy yards from the bend in the hedge. He's there.

—What are we looking for?

—The sniper.

—Oh, of course, I'd forgotten. What are the marks, Einstein? How do you know he's there?

—I know. Look, I'll give you four minutes to work your way round. Then watch for the puff of smoke.

He rang off, rummaged beneath the telephone, pulled out his old Army beret. He tugged it on, shaped it. Waited.

He crawled through the hedge, stepped onto the road, started to march, head up, arms swinging. His scalp itched under the beret as he braced himself.

Finally the shot rang out, the bullet nicking his ear as he ducked his head.

Then a volley of cross-fire and screamed orders.

He watched, fascinated, as a skylark spiralled up for real, hovering, spilling with song.

—You're a bloody fool, McKuen. But well done.

　　—If I'd had an Enfield 3, you lot could have stayed at home.

　　—We'll suggest it in the report. Like your own tank?

　　—A-T mortar would be useful.

—Mr. McKuen. Thanks for coming in. Read the report. Well done. We're grateful. Look here, how far were you intending to take this?

　　—The need arose, for you, for me. I volunteered my help. I hadn't thought any further ahead.

　　—How about something a little more ambitious?

11b

THE ARMS RAID actually took place in 1953, along with several others by the IRA. The arms were recovered, mainly by luck — their van broke down. But other, smaller raids took place later, with some arms not accounted for, including a couple of Enfield 4s with telescopic sights.

I was approached by *them*, in fact. I suppose they still had my records, and I was covered by the Official Secrets Act already, by virtue of my job in the Post Office.

It was thought the IRA might have been planning to resurrect their wartime mainland campaign. I was simply asked for advice on the psychology of snipers, choice of hides, mode of operation and so on. They were hoping not to involve the Army if at all possible.

Nothing happened. All the intelligence pointed to a border campaign, which in fact started at the end of '56, with the bombing of TA buildings, a BBC transmitter, a few pubs.

But it petered out. The Republic *spiralling up* introduced internment in the summer of '57, following that of the North; most of the leaders were rounded up, the rest demoralized.

I was thanked for my co-operation, and that, apparently, was that.

Then, a few months later, I was contacted again, asked if I would help in something more definite, and potentially more dangerous. I had nothing then to lose. I was still missing Isabelle, and didn't much care what happened to me.

I have since wondered how she fitted in to all this.

The earlier request over the arms raids seemed in retrospect to have been merely a formal ploy to establish contact, a psychological softening-up. Then a lot more fell into place. Had Isabelle been preparing me, sounding out my loyalties? Even more wildly, had she been recruiting me for some other cause, and given up over my intransigence or indifference?

Either way, it would have explained her sudden disappearance, which is what I was desperately trying to do, to the extent of clutching at straws.

On the other hand, maybe she just got tired of me.

We — I mean, Britain — had just tested our first H-bomb, in the spring of '57. There had been a number of anti-nuclear groups for some time, of course, which eventually amalgamated into CND. But a few didn't, or at least one group didn't. It called itself the Neutron Committee, and it wasn't interested in political protest or public demonstration. It meant business.

A few death threats had been sent. And they seemed remarkably well informed, both scientifically and politically.

They were followed by sabotage threats to atomic energy plants, which, given their inside knowledge, began to be taken seriously.

The first test went ahead in May as planned, on Christmas Island. It was in fact a hybrid bomb, not a true hydrogen bomb, and the test was as much of public reaction as of the bomb itself, reporters being flown out to witness the technological triumph. Further, true, tests were planned for the autumn, on other, uninhabited Pacific islands, but the precise locations of these were kept secret.

The Neutron Committee, however, located them, which pointed to inside information, or a degree of astuteness which rendered them even more dangerous.

They threatened to send a boatload of Polynesians to inhabit the islands, and claim to the press that they had always lived there. Sufficient people would be fooled to cause international embarrassment.

Neither persuasion nor threats would ever have worked; infiltration would take too long. The only possible solution was thought to be presenting them with a better propaganda coup, allowing them to think of it as *their* initiative: a high-ranking hostage opportunity.

Which is where I came in.

I gather I was to have genned up on nuclear physics, been drafted onto the team, and left vulnerable. But they couldn't get clearance, and the plan was shelved. I suspect they worried about my civilian status. I was expendable, but was I reliable? And how convincing would I have been as a nuclear scientist?

Then, in the autumn, came the Windscale fire. Three tons of uranium ablaze, fanned by the cooling fans.

A number of governmental untruths have come to light over the years, but it probably was a genuine accident.

The Neutron Committee saw its opportunity, nearer home than the South Pacific. They threatened to leak the 'fact' that it had actually been sabotage, then later claim responsibility.

It's a curious aspect of human behaviour, or at least of politicians' understanding of human behaviour, that meant the government believed it could reassure the public over an atomic accident but not over deliberate sabotage; that the public would accept an act of God but panic over an act of criminals.

Rightly or wrongly, the assessment meant that they couldn't take the risk of the sabotage claim, and, in the hope that their Pacific bomb test threat was also still operational, the hostage plan was taken down and dusted off, with some amendment.

I was, as I had thought, judged unconvincing as a

white-coat, and switched to suit-and-raincoat. I was given a government attaché case and security pass, and was driven in a chauffeured car from Whitehall to Aldermaston several times a week.

I was also given a passport, with entries to various African and Pacific countries, and America, although officially they were not co-operating with the British tests, in fact were the reason we were doing the tests, solo, at all.

Again I spent hours poring over maps, familiarizing myself with possible test sites.

In the meantime the usual Official Inquiry had been set up over the Windscale fire, to damp down the sabotage claim if it surfaced. As a stalling device, official inquiries are of course tailor-made, and that gave us a breathing space, time to sit and wait for a bite. In fact, intelligence reports had noted several number plates that came up more than randomly on our routes from Whitehall. Soon the sultry inactivity would be over.

It's difficult now to remember what a strange mixture the Fifties were of cream-and-brown cosiness and febrile speculation; how quickly after the war the country relapsed into parochial nostalgia, while facing unprecedented possibilities, most of them tied to atomic energy. Periodic scares, and relentlessly positive propaganda in editorials, from Fleet Street to parish magazines.

For myself, having tried to settle into domestic life, it

felt good to be doing something active again. The danger was a stimulant, the need for which had been reawakened. And I really *didn't* care whether I lived or died. I knew there was no possibility, for me, of falling in love again. And there seemed little else.

The possibility of death was real, despite their assurances. Why were they using, trusting, an untrained civilian? I figured the point was my expendability. They would refuse to meet any demands for my release, impressing their determination not to be deflected fractionally in their thermonuclear programme. My death would either be hushed up, or selectively reported to strengthen the government and discredit the growing disarmament movement.

But at least it would be a *specific* death. Not a wartime statistic, as it could earlier have been. An individual death. Which becomes more important the older you get.

We had worked out a route from London to Aldermaston which passed through a number of potential ambush spots, then stuck to it, varying the times of the journeys just enough to allay suspicion. I sat in the back seat of the car, leafing through 'classified' reports, my nape and spine tingling, as in the old days.

Two number plates were now cropping up regularly, one taking over from the other, leapfrogging along the route, behind us. This continued for some weeks, with no actual attempt made. London were losing interest, assuming the hostage idea hadn't been taken up after all.

I couldn't stand another anti-climax. I suggested we push them, bait them more openly.

I took a small bottle of salt water in my attaché case. A few minutes before the last projected ambush spot, I drank it.

I just held out. Then as we approached the bend, my driver stopped, I jumped out, and vomited profusely.

I sat on the verge, sitting on the case, which was chained to my wrist, looking suitably ashen.

The first car passed us. I heard it slow down beyond the bend, and reverse, as the second car approached and stopped. A man got out, ran across.

—You alright, old man?

—Touch of the collywobbles. I'll be fine.

—You'd do better to get up, walk around, relax the muscles. Here, take my arm.

—I'm fine, just need fresh air.

—I insist.

I felt the pistol scrape my shoulder blade. From the onside of the car another man got out, ran to the service car, pushed a spike under the rear tyre.

I got up, shakily, clutching the attaché case, while he held the chain, guided me to the second car. My chauffeur put on a show, reversing into the spike, getting out and shouting, as I told him to get back in and wait. It must have been convincing enough.

We reversed, mounting the verge, and pulled off round the service car, past the first car, which then followed. I was in the back seat with my captor. He leaned across and put a blindfold round my eyes, apologizing as he did so. His fingers felt dextrous, authoritative. The fingers of a surgeon, perhaps, a doctor. He reminded me in fact of my father. Especially when he checked that it was not too tight. He asked me if I still felt sick. I did, actually. He promised me we'd stop for fresh air in half an hour or so.

After the stop — at which I breathed in the needle-sharp scent of pines — we carried on driving for several hours. From the sun on my head I knew we were heading north. Otherwise, I was in the dark. We sat in silence throughout. But a strangely companionable silence.

When we eventually slowed down, I knew we were in an urban area, though quiet. Little traffic. Possibly a depressed, even derelict, area. We pulled into some sort of yard or car park, drew up alongside a wall. We both had to climb out of the onside door.

I was led through an outer door, made to wait as the door was padlocked. The door, I could feel, was half a double door, with push bars. A cinema, perhaps, theatre.

We went down a lengthy corridor into a room, where the blindfold was removed. I was in a changing room, benches, lockers. There were just the three of us, my captor, the driver, myself, but I was aware of others beyond the room, probably the occupants of the second car.

My captor — I never did discover his name — invited me to take a shower. I was grateful, although I suspected it was a way of parting me from the attaché case without violence. Although I could hardly have refused to take it off anyway. And it was important to us that they examine the passport and files. So I unlocked the chain, undressed, stepped into the shower room, turned on the first tap.

Brown, rusted water trickled through, then a current of cold water, gradually clearing. A new block of soap lay in the dish.

When I emerged from the shower room, the table in the changing room had been set — sandwiches, pot of tea, and a glass of water and some Alka Seltzer.

He said: I hope you don't mind sandwiches on your first night; there hasn't been time to cook.

The attaché case was on one of the benches, the contents piled tidily beside it. Nothing was said as to whether they had been taken in. Then, pouring the tea, he said: Tomorrow we will telephone our demands to your department. Meanwhile, please relax. How is your stomach?

I took the Alka Seltzer, in case a touch of gastric flu prove useful in the future.

We drank tea and settled down for the wait.

12a

AGAINST THE MOON-TATTERED clouds the towers stooped black, threadbare flags limp on the spires.

The pitch, long-since grown out, is discernible by the sagging goals, their nets rotted to webs. Around the perimeter, through rye and dandelion walk three figures. All three acknowledge their dewed ankles and the smell of night.

After three circuits of the ghosted pitch they turn down the crumbling tunnel, still walking three abreast. Then the middle figure is pushed ahead, into the changing room, and the door locked.

He sits on the massage table, kicks off wet shoes, lies back to plan and prowl and wait for the lassitude.

After dragging sleep, McKuen woke to the knock on the door and proffered cup of tea.

He washed in the shower, cupping his hands to catch the trickle and splash it systematically over his torso. Breakfast of cereal, served dry, and more tea. Another day's wait in the neutral zone of hope.

This was his fifth day here by his reckoning. No

response from the department. Unless his captors were holding out on him, making him sweat for their own ends or amusement.

Maybe they were trying to turn him, to send him back as a mole or sleeper. Or merely convert him. One more candle against the engulfing evil.

Yesterday afternoon's discussion had been particularly intense, Jesuitical in its twisting subtlety.

—You really believe, then, Mr. Cain, that there is nothing unethical in tampering with Nature for our own ends?

—Our very presence tampers with Nature. It's unavoidable. We trample life by breathing, eating.

—But our impact is contained by the constraints of Nature, as is the rest of the chain. But once we violate . . .

—Transcend . . .

—Those constraints, our limited destruction becomes limitless, ethically and, now, actually.

—Once we have been granted power, knowledge, we can't refuse it. It becomes a responsibility. We can only use it or hand it on. And whom we hand it to may be more unscrupulous.

—You see man as masters of the world. We see him as stewards. Experience can't be unlearned; knowledge — technical knowledge — can. It *can* be destroyed. Equations can be burnt. A hydrogen bomb is not one person's knowledge. It is a collaborative chain. Links can be removed, Mr. Cain.

—Am I to take that personally? I'm not part of the chain. I'm not a scientist.

—You administer the results. You make decisions on the use.

—I just help to choose the test sites.

—Choose *no* site.

—It's my job to choose a specific location.

—Your responsibility to choose?

—Yes.

—You just said it was your job.

—My job is my responsibility. If I didn't do it, they'd employ someone else.

—So you're passing on the responsibility, passing the buck up the chain?

—It's how democratic government works.

—But *your* responsibility, Mr. Cain, when will you take that?

—I have.

—You are wholehearted in your approval of unleashed destruction?

—It's limited. That's the point of the tests.

—Test implies uncertainty of outcome.

—That's why I have the job of finding suitable locations.

—The rest is left to the scientists?

—It's their job.

—Exactly, Mr. Cain.

McKuen chewed on the cereal, gritty against his gums. He suddenly saw a way out, a path of salvation. *He* was not making the choice. The choice was made by Cain. Whatever decisions he made were made in character, so to speak, left him personally untouched, inviolable.

During the morning exercise, which he would normally have enjoyed, all he wanted was to be back in the locker room, alone, to work out the possible moves in the afternoon's debate, assuming it carried on from where they had left off; planning out when and how to concede.

After lunch, of Spam and a tomato and the inevitable tea, his captor entered the room as usual, unfolded a chair.

—These tests of yours, Mr. Cain.

McKuen groaned aloud.

—They're not *my* tests.

—You admitted responsibility for them.

—For their location.

—You approve of their *fact*.

—I have no choice in that.

—We've been through that. You were, then, I take it, conscripted to the job.

—Seconded.

—These tests, Mr. Cain. What would constitute the outcome of a successful test, in your view? The abolition of the bomb?

—The predictability of its effect.

—Which would allow, encourage, its use?

—The successful bomb is the one that *isn't* used.

—Sufficient that it scare enough people into submission? The V2s, Mr. Cain. You remember them?

—I was mostly overseas for the duration.

—There were rumours, scare stories, for months beforehand. But they were only effective when they were used.

—They were still conventional bombs. This is a very different concept. You have seen the results.

—I have, Mr. Cain. Weapons that cannot be used. A novel logic, as you say. Who should have these bombs, Mr. Cain?

—As few countries as possible.

—But if they're designed not to be used, *all* should have them.

—Then, inevitably, they will be used.

—My point, Mr. Cain. Is that why America is pressing us to give up ours, rely on theirs?

—You're remarkably well-informed.

—We make it our business. You don't agree with them, then? You want the weapons limited, but insist *we* have them. Should America?

—We can hardly prevent it.

—But our own? We can prevent that. Voluntarily set the example. Rely on American cover.

—We can hardly be expected to surrender our independence.

—America is not a reliable ally?

—I didn't say that.

—You find yourself in something of a cleft, Mr. Cain. The novelty of the new logic has not yet sunk in. Maybe it will do so overnight.

McKuen through the evening, the night, examined the arguments step by step, searching for the chink, the logical burrow that would allow a reversal of position, a negotiated capitulation. It still eluded him.

Maybe they were right: the new logic permitted sudden reversals. Maybe, as McKuen *or* Cain he could revise his views in good faith. Extreme conditions affect normal chemical reactions. Would the intensity of a hydrogen bomb not qualify?

Perhaps he should put the onus on them; say he was unsure of his position, allow *them* to find the weaknesses, the cracks, erode his foundation.

He woke from shallow, scratchy sleep at the turn of the lock. It was not the usual henchman.

—Tea, Mr.Cain. And news. A reply from your masters.

Tentative, circumspect, as expected. But the beginning of a negotiation.

—What's your asking price?

—Good God, Mr. Cain, you took us for mercenaries all this time? Bandits, after all our discussions?

—Abandonment of the tests? Complete disarmament?

—We are idealists, Mr. Cain. That doesn't make us naive. We want open air. A breeze of debate in the stuffy corridors of Whitehall. Publicity for the arguments. Informed public opinion.

—Has there been any news coverage of my abduction?

—The power of the Press? Again, Mr. Cain, we are not naive. The Press is easily hushed. Intone the phrases Official Secret, Government Security, and editors roll over in a patriotic blush.

—But there are several protest groups active. There's even talk of them amalgamating, organizing public protests.

—Whatever press coverage they get will be to discredit them. They are outsiders. They will be portrayed as cranks, pacifists, sandal-wearing, carrot-juice drinkers. Debate will only be opened up by insider dissent.

—You wish me to be that Insider? Is that what the dialectical chats were for?

—You, Mr. Cain? Heavens, no. You have made your position clear.

—My position may change, on reflection.

—We would only have your word for that. No, your job is to remain here until the debate starts.

—And if it doesn't?

—We are patient people. And prepared to make sacrifices for the overall objective. If your position really is changing, your sacrifice will be as voluntary as ours. Besides, we have further ways of stimulating debate.

—The Windscale accident? You're still going to use that? There's a government inquiry already in progress. It will confirm the accidental nature of the event.

—To the non-cynical. And it will take time, as you know yourself, Mr. Cain. A year, two years?

—Your claims will be hushed up, like my captivity.

—The accident is already known to the public. Your 'abduction' is not.

—Tell me, were you actually involved?

—You're not sure yourself of the accident theory?

—Nobody knows for sure yet what caused it. Sabotage has been suggested by some of the science chaps.

—We have ethics, Mr. Cain. They are the basis of our cause. To deliberately poison the air, water, milk? Self-defeating logic. A note of warning, though. Under certain circumstances, our ethics allow injury, to the non-inno-cent bystander.

—Do I take that as another threat?

—Take it as guidance.

McKuen was almost amused at the irony: having changed his views, he was no longer in a position to act on them. And they were the views of himself, McKuen, rather than Cain's. For wasn't the case the same as his campaign after the war? His own vendetta against injustice, bullying? Which in fact was what had landed him in this position in the first place.

His change of heart, if indeed it was a change, for he hadn't really examined his views beforehand, had been in good faith.

And had come too late.

There was only one way to convince his captors that his views were genuine. He finished his lunch and waited calmly for the afternoon's ideological duel.

—Mr. Cain, we've known that all along. You still believe us to be naive? You were never a convincing civil servant. You lack the suavity. Besides, it was all too easy. You were so obviously a bone thrown to the dogs. But since you were so neatly tossed into our lap, it would have been churlish not to have taken advantage. Rest assured, though, *we* don't view humans as bones. You are a human being, of infinite worth, like everyone else. And as such, valuable, useful, to us. However, the osteological valuation of your bosses could lead to problems in the negotiations — or lack of.

The knowledge McKuen had had from the beginning now had the force of the experiential: he was alone. Even his operator probably didn't know his location, and certainly no one else. The blanket secrecy would absorb any cry he made, any attempt by his captors to draw attention to his plight. He could effectively vanish. Maybe he already had. A rumoured accident on his holiday trip, his cover for the work, would be enough.

In his evening exercise he was extra vigilant, noting every glimmer of light from the walls and fences, gaps in the doors beyond the rusted turnstiles. He could see nothing.

They went back down the tunnel to the changing room. As they did so, a possibility opened up.

He waited, after the lock was turned, for the footsteps to die, then began to check his hunch.

Some of the enamelled lockers were still there, silent as museum sarcophagi. Others had evidently been removed, leaving grimed outlines on the floor and walls. He counted both lockers and spaces. Fifteen. So despite the size of the room it must have been the home team's only. Which meant another room for the visiting team, on the other side of the tunnel.

He went into the shower room. He followed the pipe along the wall, tapped and listened. His guess was correct; the two shower rooms were adjacent, presumably below the tunnel. A wire grille ran across the top of the dividing wall.

He just had time before supper to work on the screws with his nail clippers, push the grille back into its place with finger pressure.

He ate the supper slowly, knowing the water wouldn't be turned on until nine o'clock.

He listened for the splutter in the pipe, left his jacket folded on the bench, took a chair.

He undressed, turned on the shower, reached and pulled away the grille as the water coughed through the pipe.

He pushed his bundled clothing through, wet and soaped himself under the shower, eased himself painfully through the opening, pulling the grille back into position before dropping to the floor.

He tried the shower this side — it worked. He sluiced off the soap and dirt, pulled on his clothes.

He came out of the shower into the other, darkened changing room. A shape loomed out. A greyed towel on a hook. He carefully tried the door — it was unlocked. He listened, crept out, up the tunnel onto the pitch, ran up the touchline and vaulted the turnstile.

The only way out was to kick through the door, but a single well-aimed kick would do it. He carefully chose the spot midway between the hinges, pivoted on his heel.

A flash tore across, blinding. As he slowly lowered his

forearm, blinking, he found himself impaled in the cross-beams of the floodlights.

12b

I NEVER DID FIND out his name, although I came to know a lot else about him, to know him well.

Despite the impeccability of his English, in both speech and demeanour, he had actually been born in Austria. He was one of twins, near-identical. When his parents split up, he came here with his English mother. His brother and father stayed in Austria.

He went to pre-war Cambridge, doing philosophy, briefly under Wittgenstein, at whose insistence he switched to engineering. His brother became a physicist, ended up conscripted into German atomic research. After the war and his de-Nazification, he was drafted into the American research programme.

The brothers became close again, mine — my captor — spending a few years over there, during which time they had intense debates about the morality of the research.

The brothers looking so alike, as a way of convincing him of the value of what he was doing, the physicist brother lent him his identity papers and passes, giving access *burrow* to some of the research establishments.

It made him more opposed, but also gave him valuable background knowledge for his later campaign.

That was his story.

Certainly he seemed authoritative in his discussions. And deeply troubled. I think he felt guilty twice over, guilty on his brother's behalf, personally responsible.

As an only child, that's not something I could understand. But his commitment impressed me. It wasn't ideological.

We talked at length. He wasn't trying to brainwash me; they were merely a civilized way of whiling away the time until my department responded, which I knew from the start they had no intention of doing.

We had, apart from my lack of a twin brother, a lot in common. His father too had been a doctor, a neurologist in Vienna, similarly distant and disappointed in his son. He himself was a keen cross-country runner.

He'd spent the war over here, interned to begin with, on the Isle of Wight, then volunteer recruitment into weapons development, after lengthy probing of his loyalties.

I challenged him on the irony of that. He said they were still conventional weapons, and since they had to be used — he fully supported the war on Hitler — they should be made as safe as possible. He'd developed a number of safety improvements: to the pins on hand grenades, recoil dampers, smoother transmission on tank tracks.

We discussed rifles a good deal. His father had been

a hunter, with a collection of antique firearms as well as modern hunting pieces.

We discussed the conditions on the post-war continent. I told him what I had seen of vengeance and greed and absolute desperation; that I had been involved in unofficial relief missions.

I had to be careful not to give myself away, but we had reached a point where I suspect it wouldn't have mattered. Even so, I had to try to talk and think in character, whether I agreed with him or not.

I didn't, on the whole. Having seen at first hand the devastation caused by bullying, I believed, still believe, that the only thing to stop a bully is a bigger bully. In the case of nations, it means bigger weapons. I could see his arguments, logically, but it wasn't just patriotism, my rejection of them.

I put my case cogently, I hope, but with decreasing vehemence, crumbling resolve.

The fact was, I felt sorry for him. I admired his sincerity. Wasn't he, after all, trying the same lone mission I had attempted? I knew that whatever the outcome of my abduction, eventually he would be found, probably hanged.

I offered at one point to put his case, plead his sincerity. Assuming the government responded (I had, as I said, to act in character). But I meant it. He treated me well.

We would eat together, the four of us. We would exercise together, just he and I. We scythed out a running track round the perimeter of the football pitch, paced each other.

And at the end of the day, we prayed together. At least, he prayed, I listened, non-committally, but he insisted, and insisted we do it kneeling. Which didn't do my knee much good.

13a

—Always leave a man a loophole, Mr. Cain. It narrows down the points of surveillance. I thought you'd be getting desperate by now. Despite your protestations of agreement, your conversion to our cause.

—As it happens, I was beginning to agree. But it wasn't going to affect my treatment, was it?

—You've been well-treated, Mr. Cain.

—I'm not complaining. But you've blocked yourself into a corner, and me with you. I have no influence over the government.

—And in the meantime, as a prisoner of war, you are duty-bound to escape, and if it fails, attempt it again. Entirely right. A man must live by his conscience. We have to respect that. And act accordingly.

They took McKuen by gunpoint to the visitors' changing room. The light was now on. The room was bare but for coconut matting on which lay scaffolding pipes tied together at two-inch intervals.

Another pole was held behind his knees as he was forced to kneel, and his wrists tied to his ankles. He was lifted and pushed until he knelt on the poles on the coconut mat.

— Buddhist monks in the Middle Ages used to kneel on gravel to concentrate their minds, Mr. Cain. We thought this a little less mediaeval. Darkness they also found conducive to contemplation.

The light suddenly snapped off, but the pain jumping across his synapses confused his reflexes; he couldn't be sure for several seconds that he hadn't gone blind.

He was aware of movement, worked out that they were leaving him, heard the distant click of the lock through the curtains of pain, felt the darkness congeal as he blacked out.

He came to slumped to his right, the angle of his legs increasing the torque of the pole on his thighs. He adjusted to the pain, which had subtly changed, and to the silence beyond the roaring of his ears. He found in the new position that he could move his feet, which took the strain off his ankles. His fingers were tingling from the tightness of the ropes but he retained some dexterity.

He closed his ankles, moved one forward, fiddled for the knot. He recognized it as a clove hitch, began patiently to find the end, reverse the loops, half-inch by half-inch.

The other was easier as his arm was free, but still

tauntingly slow. He had no idea how long he had been unconscious, how soon they'd come back.

Finally it freed, and he pulled away the pole, lay on his side. Slowly he regained movement in his legs, while he thought out his position.

The knot was elementary, easy to undo compared with others. He remembered the phrase, leave a man a loophole. Were the knots also a loophole? Where did they expect him?

The only way out was through the replaced grille back through the home showers. That's where they'd expect him. There was no other choice. He'd have to double bluff, which entailed a diversion.

He rolled himself across into the shower room, took off his shirt, folded and patted it down over the drain, pulled himself up, turned on the taps one by one, praying the water was still on.

The combined outlets increased the water pressure to almost normal. As the level rose he wrenched off the grille with the scaffold pole, pulled himself through, the pole after him.

He crawled across the home changing room to the outer door, dragging the pole. He had a few minutes before the water built up in the other room. He measured up the empty locker nearest the door wall, pushed it a few inches, overturned it. It was now almost flush with the wall.

He jammed the end of the scaffold into the gap, and leaning against the wall, held it across the door. Waited.

He heard the shout that meant the water was now seeping under the other door, heard the key turned, the door pushed open, the splashing steps.

As he expected, one of them had already guessed his way of escape through the shower, was pushing against his door. He braced the pole against the shoving, then suddenly pulled the end free, dived onto the tumbling figure.

He pulled the gun from his grasp, rolled over several times, brought the gun round in a single reflex. He fired once into the far wall.

—Alright, Mr. Cain, you already have the advantage of me.

—Call the other two in.

He got slowly to his feet, the gun now aimed at his captor's head.

He motioned the others into the shower, indicated to his captor to precede him through the door, locked it after them.

—Keys to the car.

The keys jangled across the concrete floor.

—You'll be going alone, I take it? Tell me, Mr. Cain, do you still agree with our views, or was that a ploy?

—I meant it.

—So you are still in a cleft. Do you join us now, from

choice, on your own terms? Or do you suppress your opinions, go back to your job, do your duty? Let me suggest. If you're sincere, you're worth more to us in your job, putting our case. Your conscience will be clear either way. Your only dilemma now is whether to kill me. Only you can decide that. But decide carefully. Only you have to live with the decision.

McKuen picked up the keys, tossed them at him.

—I don't drive.

The car was parked hard up against the stadium wall.

McKuen waited as the other opened the passenger door, reached back to open the rear door, slid across to the driver's seat.

McKuen wound down the front window, slammed both doors shut, leaned into the car.

—You're not coming, Cain?

—I'm passing the buck. It's your decision. Turn yourself in, or drive into the distance. If *you're* sincere, you'll find the nearest police station, give yourself up. I imagine there'll be sufficient publicity for your cause once I speak to the press. Up to you, though.

—Afraid of the choice, Cain? You can only postpone it. You'll eventually *fall* off the fence.

McKuen put his left hand into his trouser pocket, attempted to relax. His fingers, fidgeting, closed round a coin, a florin. He pressed it into his palm, smoothed the other side with his finger, let it drop, turned it round.

He felt himself caught between two force fields, oscillating between futures. He wanted to go back inside the stadium, out onto the field into the long grass, lie burrowed in the stasis.

—Come with me, Cain.

The words sounded simultaneously distant and inside his skull. He flexed his hand in his pocket, plucked at the florin, fired.

The recoil caught him off guard.

The bullet, outdistancing any paradox, tunnelled through the years.

13b

IT BECAME INCREASINGLY obvious, not just to me (I knew already), but to him too, that the department, the government, would not respond, that the whole point of the exercise was their non-response, their refusal to strike deals, even to talk to dissenters.

I felt for him. He'd backed himself into a corner from which there was no escape. For what were his options? Let me go? I knew too much about him. If the government weren't interested in saving *me*, they would hardly consider any plea of mine on *his* behalf.

Shoot me? A less decent man would have justified that in terms of the rightness of the cause. But our wary rapport, I felt, ruled that out.

Lock me in, drive off, leave an anonymous tip-off as to my whereabouts?

A possibility, but a definite defeat, a failure of his cause, and therefore of *fidgeting* his life.

His solution surprised even me. He brought me in my breakfast, joined me in a mug of tea, then handed me his gun.

The onus was on me; and I hadn't a clue.

He'd left the door unlocked. I slipped the gun into my jacket pocket, went to find him. He was out on the pitch, walking rather than running.

We walked together round the path we'd cleared.

I asked him if he still intended to claim the Windscale accident as sabotage, in which case he'd need to get in before the inquiry was finished. He said: That rather depends on you.

I said he should go ahead. No harm would be done, no one would be hurt.

I felt no further loyalty to a department which cared nothing for me. And there was no longer any point in acting in character. We discussed how to float it, which journalists to approach, which papers to tip off. His grasp of the technicalities of the accident was near-professional; he could make the sabotage claim sound convincing. But then . . .

We'd stopped at the far end, by the turnstiles. He had a distinctive gesture, a mannerism, when talking, of holding up his cupped hands as if weighing in the balance immeasurable pros and cons. He'd stopped talking, but his hands were still suspended in mid-balance. I looked at them.

I remembered the touch of his hands as he put on,

later removed, the blindfold, in the car. A doctor's touch.
I thought of my father. And . . .
I shot him.

14a

THE SUN WAS long down but the twilight lingered. McKuen pushed on through the grass, losing the track, leaning more heavily on his stick as the gradient changed. Its ferrule pierced the turf, biting into the chalk.

He had made the incline, could feel the down falling away before him, allowed himself a rest. He lowered himself onto the dry turf, slowly straightened his ruined knee.

The pain as he did so sharpened but was still a calmative, a distracting focus. He opened his jacket, spread it so he was clear of the bulge, lay back.

In the valley a screech owl called, clarified in the thinning air. Its shadow passed over, scuttling the rabbits, was gone.

The gods had withdrawn. He was alone.

He felt the air thin even more, threatening to draw him up, even gravity no longer dependable, felt he was held to the earth by only the weight in his pocket.

The last of the light drained from the sky. The domes of

the far Downs, the puff of trees against the horizon, were indistinct, absorbed by the dark. He tried to concentrate on the shape of his past, the succession of created selves, but they too were shadowy, unlimnable. Lying back on the fragrant turf, he could find no purchase—there was only the present: the brush of grass and hawkbit on his cheek, scent of crushed geranium, the silence of the owl's absence. And down the slope, in the longer grass, the winking burn of the glow-worms.

He needed to gather in the energy for a last reinvention, to redefine an amorphous future. But there was no light left, no reserve of energy.

He rolled over, pushed himself onto his knees, slowly hauled himself up the stick, stood swaying a moment on the cusp, half turned. Then step-by-step started down the slope.

He felt the longer grass whip his ankles. The green flares of the glow-worms led him on, led him deeper, deeper into himself.

He reached the edge of the chalk stream, now in midsummer reduced to a whisper.

His life too was reduced, to a single decision, a decision he knew he needn't make for himself. He had merely to surrender to the bias of the weight in his jacket.

He stepped into the stream bed, gauged its current,

followed it down into the thickening dark until he found a suitable hide among the last wild orchids.

14b

Surrender to the bias of the weight in my pocket. My God. Is that what my life has been reduced to? Amateurish purple?

Look, I don't so much mind my life being borrowed. It's what novelists do. They have to make a living. I understand that. And besides, I can correct it, put the record straight.

What I do mind is my death being stolen. It hasn't happened yet! How else could I have given that bloody interview? *Unsung Lives, Unsung Heroes,* some stupid bloody series title. I couldn't bring myself to listen to the broadcast. Vanity and money, the oldest traps out.

But I tried. To be honest.

Well, I suppose you could say in a sense it occurred. A death is an end of a life. And I dropped from view, disappeared when I changed identity. That life was over.

I requested — demanded — the department's help. They couldn't refuse. I convinced them I was still in danger from the Neutron Committee. And I *had*, overtly, fulfilled my assignment.

A new name. New home, new start. Maybe not so much a new life as the chance to regain the life I would have led had the war not distorted it, buckled the contours, as it did for all *absorbed by the dark* my generation.

In actual fact it was easier than I expected. Like holding a dual passport. I could slip between lives, in memory, as I pleased.

For what was important I'd retained. Life is not the plot, it's the pattern of moments, immediately insignificant—the sun on your neck and the scent of gorse, smell of chalk and desk wood, of oil and rubber, the taste of smoke, star wind at midnight, a woman's breast.

These form the core of your being, which doesn't really change through the outer mutations.

I was at first dismayed, excited, at the thought of a fresh start, the chance to be whatever I chose, to have a clean slate to write on.

But it's never like that. The force field settles back, the clean slate proves only a palimpsest and you find yourself retracing old texts.

Alright, yes, there's the remorse, that's there, it's always there, it becomes a part of you. It grows inside, a stone, a weight knocking you off orbit. But you adjust, the contours remould, your orbit subtly alters, you carry on.

I've lived with it all these years, as I have the wartime deaths, the deaths of my parents, others, the losses. It's part of the pattern, of the past.

Yes, there have been times, there are times in everyone's life . . . Look, there are two natural defences against suicide — cowardice and curiosity. I've always had both. This isn't my death. I don't have the vocation.

Our own death is the one we live with, the one we imagine. The real thing will no doubt take us by surprise, in unexpected form; that doesn't matter, it's too late then to matter. But the death we live with, the one that shapes our life —

Mine has altered somewhat over the years. Now, finally, it's a gentle ebb to the closing bars of Mahler's *Ninth*; slip away unmourned, drift into the dark. That's how I define myself now, what I live by. I'm not prepared to lose that. I can't . . . have it violated.

I'm on painkillers most of the time now, for my knee, and alright, yes, sometimes the temptation is there to up the dosage, but always there's one more day, curiosity about tomorrow.

Look, I don't even know where the gun is, whether it works.

15

I'VE BEEN LOOKING through my old maps, maps of the Downs, reading the contours, looking for the spot he had in mind.

It may not even exist — it's probably fictitious, like most of the book.

I've located a spot that seems to fit. A valley with a small village, a chalk stream. Now a Site of Special Scientific Interest on account of its wild orchids.

It's not far from some of my old cycle training routes. I've been riding these again in my mind, retracing from memory the bends and dips, climbs and flats. A life ago.

A shame I didn't move up here after the war. Tackled some of the Pennine climbs. The equal of some Alpine cols. The training would have stood me in good stead. Maybe I'd have made a career on the Continent after all. Life could have been so different.

At any rate, I like it up here now; I'm settled.

I have decided on a holiday. A weekend break, no more.

Train fare and two nights in Brighton for senior citizens. Within half an hour of the spot on the map.

It's been quite a walk from where the taxi dropped me. But there's time. It's still afternoon, the sun scorching my back.

I can appreciate now what he meant by the trope of the bias. I find myself unconsciously leaning against the weight of the gun.

I've no idea whether it would even fire now. But that doesn't matter. I just need to live through it in my mind, free myself from the gravitational pull, return to orbit. Reclaim my death.

Dark now. But no glow-worms. Maybe they're extinct here. I'll have to imagine them. And the chalk stream's dry.

I've found the orchids.

I played the Mahler on my Walkman last night, in my room. I can still hear it in my head, against the busy silence.

The orchids burn into the dark like torches. I'm amazed they still exist in the wild, even protected.

The turf is still warm, teeming with life. Yet the net result of all the frenzied activity is peace. How strange.

Lie back, let my mind go blank. Like those moments in the war, the lull in the engagement when you disengaged, floated away.

But I'm here for a purpose.

Take out the pistol, check the safety catch is on, hold it to my head.

Break the spell.

It's the first time I've handled it since I used it.

I told the department I'd thrown it into the under-growth in panic.

All those years.

His face swims up, clear, breaking from the depths. I see him, see the surprise on his face as he hears the hammer trip. Features pin-sharp yet bleached out, overexposed. Shock, I guess.

All the years, all the memories he's been denied, while life went on. My life.

The others too. From the war. A long head-start in their acclimatization.

What happened to them, where are their remains?

I'm curious. A curiosity I've never felt before. Is it remorse in disguise?

I'm curious as to where they are now—the bodies, the

souls — what they went through, the stages and degrees of death, the slow or quick intensity. Is this remorse?

Could any of it have been different?

No, this is not self-justification. We have choices, responsibility. But the context of our choices is beyond control. Our choices are constrained.

    'The last decision left to him.' But what if, having made his last, preordained decision, the gun had failed?

    The ending, I remember, was left open.

I still don't know if the gun works. So my decision too depends on outside factors, on chance.

I'm waiting for an owl-hoot.

Slip off the safety catch.

Lightning Source UK Ltd.
Milton Keynes UK
UKOW04f0355210715

255541UK00002B/16/P